SHIELD OF DEATH

Rick heard the panic in Lisa's voice: "Skull Leader, evacuate your team at once—the barrier is about to chain react. Evacuate!"

Rick, Max, and Ben thought their Battloids through an about-face. Beyond the rim of the Zentraedi warship they could see the barrier transubstantiate: what appeared as the selfsame shield was in fact shot through and through with submolecular death.

Rick watched as radiation gauges came to life in the cockpit. He raised his teammates on the tac net and told them to clear out on the double.

Behind them the shield expanded, its internal colors shifting from green through yellow and orange to deadly red; then after a blinding flash of silent white light, the shield was gone. In its place a hot pink hemisphere began to form, an umbrella of horror fifty miles wide.

Published by Ballantine Books:

THE ROBOTECH™ SERIES

THE SENTINELS™ SERIES

ROBOTECH™ #4:

BATTLEHYMN

Jack McKinney

A Del Rey Book

BALLANTINE BOOKS • NEW YORK

A Del Rey Book
Published by Ballantine Books

Library of Congress Catalog Card Number: 86-91635

ISBN 0-345-34137-6

Manufactured in the United States of America

First Edition: March 1987
Eighth Printing: April 1990

Cover Art by David Schleinkofer

FOR GABRIELA "GABBY" ARANDA

■–■–■–■–■–:■–.■.–■–■–■–■–■–■–■–■–■–■–■

CHAPTER
ONE

As far as I'm concerned [Gloval] has already disobeyed his orders; I'd urge the council to proceed with a court-martial if I could only come up with someone to replace him. What do you think, [name withheld], perhaps I could talk [Admiral] Hayes into accepting the position and kill two birds with one stone? ...This issue of the civilians aboard the SDF-1 has turned into a real mess. Personally, I consider them expendable—along with Gloval, along with the whole ship, if you want to know the truth. Let's face facts: The thing has already outlived its purpose. You and I are where we wanted to be. Why not give the aliens their damn ship and send them back where they belong?

Senator Russo, personal correspondence (source withheld)

THERE WAS SOMETHING NEW IN THE COOL SUMMER night skies of 2012 ... You remember sitting on the back-yard swing, hands tightly gripping the galvanized chains, slender arms extended and head tossed all the way back, gazing up into the immeasurable depths of that black magic, teasing your young mind with half-understood riddles of space and time. All of a sudden, your gaze found movement there where none should have existed, as if an entire constellation had uprooted and launched itself on an impromptu journey across the cosmos. Your

1

heart was beating fast, but your eyes continued to track that mystery's swift passage toward the distant horizon, even though you were watching it upside down now and in danger of toppling backward off the swing. A screen door slammed, its report a signal that your cries had been heard, your father and his friends beside you trying to follow the rapid flow of your words, your shaking forefinger, pointing to unmoving starfields. "Past your bedtime," your father said, and off you went. But you crept down the wide carpeted staircase later on, silently, invisibly, and heard them in the library talking in low tones, using words you couldn't fully comprehend but in a way that proved you weren't imagining things. You'd glimpsed the fortress, a heavenly city returned from the past, massive enough to occultate the stars ... savior or harbinger of dark prophecies, your father's friends couldn't decide which, but "a sign of the times" in either case. Like blue moons, unexplained disappearances, rumors of giants that were on their way to get you ... And on the front page of the following day's newspaper you saw what the night had kept from you: a mile-high roboid figure, propelled by unknown devices twice its own height above a stunned city, erect, legs straight, arms bent at the elbow, held out like those of a holy man or magician in a calming gesture of peace or surrender. It reminded you of something at the edge of memory, an image you wouldn't summon forth until much later, when fire rained from the sky, your night world annihilated by light ...

* * *

In direct violation of United Earth Defense Council dictates, Captain Gloval had ordered the SDF-1 airborne. It was not the first time he had challenged the wisdom of the Council, nor would it be the last.

The dimensional fortress had remained at its landing site in the Pacific for two long months like an infant in a wading pool, the supercarriers *Daedalus* and *Prometheus* that were her arms positioned out front like toys in the ocean waves. And indeed, Gloval often felt as though his superiors on the Council had been treating him like a child since the fortress's return to Earth. Two years of being chased through the solar system by a race of alien giants, only to be made to feel like unwanted relatives who had simply dropped in for a visit. Gloval had a full understanding of the Council's decisions from a military point of view, but those men who sat in judgment were overlooking one important element—or, as Gloval had put it to them, 56,000 important elements: the one-time residents of Macross Island who were onboard his ship. Circumstance had forced them to actively participate in this running space battle with the Zentraedi, but there was no reason now for their continued presence; they had become unwilling players in a game of global politics that was likely to have a tragic end.

There had already been more than 20,000 deaths; how many more were required to convince the Council to accede to his demands that the civilians be allowed to disembark?

The Council's reasoning was far from specious, it was

crazed, rooted in events that had transpired years before, but worse still, rooted in a mentality Gloval had hoped he had seen the last of. Even now the commander found that he could still embrace some of the arguments put forth in those earlier times—the belief that it was prudent to keep secret from the masses any knowledge of an impending alien attack. Secrecy had surrounded reconstruction of the dimensional fortress and the development of Robotech weaponry, the transfigurable Veritech fighters and the Spartans and Gladiators. This was the "logic of disinformation": There was a guiding purpose behind it. But the Council's current stance betrayed an inhumanity Gloval hadn't believed possible. To explain away the disappearance of the 75,000 people of Macross, the military had announced that shortly after the initial lift-off of the SDF-1, a volcanic eruption on the order of Krakatoa had completely destroyed the island. To further complicate matters, GIN, the Global Intelligence Network, spread rumors to the effect that in reality a guerrilla force had invaded the island and detonated a thermonuclear device. *Global Times Magazine* was then coerced into publishing equally unreal investigative coverage of a supposed cover-up by GIN, according to which the actual cause of the deaths on Macross was disease.

Just how any of these stories could have functioned to *alleviate* worldwide panic was beyond Gloval; the Council might just as easily have released the truth: that an experiment in hyperspace relocation had inadvertently ended with the dematerialization of the island. As it stood, however, the Council was locked into its own lies:

75,000 killed by a volcanic explosion/guerrilla invasion/ virus. Therefore, these thousands could not be allowed to "reappear"—return from the dead was an issue the Council was not ready to deal with.

The 56,000 survivors had to remain virtual prisoners aboard the SDF-1.

And if the Robotech Defense Force should win this war against the Zentraedi? Gloval had asked the Council. What then? How was the Council going to deal with the victorious return of the SDF-1 *and* the return of the dead? Couldn't they see how misguided they were?

Of course, it was a rhetorical question.

Gloval's real concern was that the Council didn't consider victory an acceptable scenario.

Which is why he had taken it upon himself to launch the SDF-1. He was going to focus attention on the civilians one way or another...

There was panic on the ground and panic in the voice of the Aeronautics Command controller.

"NAC. ground control to SDF-1 bridge: Come in immediately...NAC. ground control to SDF-1 bridge: Come in immediately, over!"

On the bridge of the dimensional fortress there were suppressed grins of satisfaction. Captain Gloval put a match to his pipe, disregarding Sammie's reminders. He let a minute pass, then signaled Claudia from the command chair to respond to the incoming transmission.

"SDF-1 bridge to NAC. ground control, I have Captain Gloval. Go ahead, over."

Gloval drew at his pipe and blew a cloud toward the overhead monitors. He could just imagine the scene below: the eyes of Los Angeles riveted on his sky spectacle. He had ordered Lang and astrogation to utilize the newly revamped antigrav generators to secure and maintain a low-level fly-by, and so the enormous triple ports of the foot thrusters were scarcely a mile above the streets. There would be no mistaking this for some Hollywood stunt. And not only were people getting their first look at the airborne SDF-1, but also of the formerly top-secret mecha that flew along with her—fighters, Guardians, and Battloids hovering and circling a mile-high bipedal Robotechnological marvel. Forget the majestic colors of those sunset clouds, Gloval wanted to tell them. Here was something really worth photographing!

"Captain Gloval, low flights over population centers have been strictly prohibited except in extreme emergencies."

Gloval reached forward and picked up the handset. "This *is* an emergency. We must maintain a low-altitude holding pattern. Our gravity control system is not perfected, and the lives of our 56,000 civilian detainees are in jeopardy."

Lisa Hayes turned from her station to throw him a conspiratorial wink.

"But sir, you're causing a panic down here. Increase your altitude and fly out over the ocean immediately. It's imperative."

I have them where I want them! Gloval said to himself.

"I will comply with your order if you can give me permission to disembark these civilians."

The speakers went silent; when the controller returned, there was incredulity and urgency in his voice.

"Sir, that's impossible. Orders from UEDC headquarters state that *no one* is to leave your ship. We have no authority to countermand those orders. You must leave this area at once."

It was time to let some of the anger show. Gloval shouted, "I will not rest until those orders are changed!"

He slammed the handset back into its cradle and leaned back into the chair. Vanessa had swiveled from her screen to study him; he knew what was on her mind and granted her the liberty to speak freely.

"Sir, isn't it dangerous to be making threats while we're on the aircom net?"

Claudia exchanged looks with Gloval and spoke for him.

"This fortress is a symbol of the Council's strength," she told Vanessa. "If it gets out that the captain is resisting orders, the Council would lose face—"

"And there's a chance," Lisa added, "that our communication *was* being monitored." She turned to Gloval. "Isn't that true, Captain?"

Gloval left the chair and walked forward to the curved bay. The cityscape was spread out beneath the ship; Veritechs flew in formation, and great swirls and billows of lavender and orange sunset clouds filled the sky.

"I'm prepared to keep the SDF-1 here until we *are* monitored, Lisa." He turned to face Claudia and the others. "I don't think there's much chance that the Council will reverse its decision. But politicians can sometimes be helpful, and it's possible that someone in the government will get wind of this, see an opportunity, and step in."

"But the Council isn't going to like your tactics, sir," said Vanessa.

Gloval turned back to the bay.

"Even if I face prosecution, this is something I must do. Civilians have no place onboard this ship. No place in this war."

But for the time being the SDF-1 was stuck with its civilians. However, it had been outfitted with a reworked shield system. Dr. Lang had dismantled the pin-point barrier and liberated the lambent energy which animated it—the same energy which had materialized with the disappearance of the spacefold generators some time ago. His team of Robotechnicians had then reanalyzed that alien fire, careful to avoid past mistakes, tamed and cajoled it, and fashioned a newly designed harness for it. Where the former system relied on manually operated maneuverable photon discs that were capable of covering only specific portions of the fortress (hence the name "pin-point" system), the reworked design was omnidirectional, allowing for full coverage. It did share some of the weaknesses of its prototype, though, in that activation of the system drained energy from the weapons systems, and full coverage was severely time-limited.

If only the personnel of the fortress could have been similarly outfitted . . . but who has yet designed a shield system for the heart, a protective barrier, pin-point or otherwise, for the human soul?

Roy Fokker was dead.

The VT pilots of Skull Team had their own way of dealing with combat deaths: The slain pilot simply never was. Men from Vermilion or Indigo might approach them in Barracks C or belowdecks in the *Prometheus* and say: "Sorry to hear about Roy," or "Heard that Roy tuned out." And they would look them square in the eye or turn to one of their Skull teammates and ask flatly, "Roy who?" some might think the skull were kidding with them and press the question, but the response remained the same: "Roy who?" Nobody broke the pact, nobody spoke of Roy, then or now. Roy simply never was.

Except in the privacy of their quarters or the no-man's-land of their tortured memories and dreams. Then a man could let loose and wail or rage or throw out the same questions humankind has been asking since that first murder, the first death at the hands of another, the one that set the pattern for all that followed.

Perhaps that shell game the Skull Team played with death had found its way to the bridge, or maybe it was just that Fokker's death was too painful to discuss—the first one that hit home—but in any case no one brought it up. Claudia and Rick were each separately cocooned in sorrow no one saw fit to disturb. Kim and Sammie talked about how sorry they felt for Claudia, knowing how much she missed Fokker, knowing that underneath that brave front she was torn up. But neither woman ever approached her with those feelings. Even Lisa seemed at a loss. That afternoon she had followed Claudia to the mess hall, hesitant at the door, as if afraid to intrude on her friend's grief... Did it occur to her that Claudia and Rick—the lieutenant at the observation deck rail and Claudia seated not fifteen feet away— might have been able to help each other through it, or was Lisa also one of the speechless walking wounded, wounds in her own heart reopened, wounds that had been on the mend until Fokker's death?

It was Rick she approached that afternoon, the City of Angels spread out below the observation deck like some Robotech circuit board. Rick looked drawn and pale, recuperating but still weak from his own brush with death from wounds he had suffered indirectly *at her own hand*. But there was no mention of Roy, although it was plain enough to read in his dark eyes the devastation he felt. And the more she listened to him, the deeper she looked into those eyes, the more fearful she became; it was as though all light had left him, as though his words rose from a hollow center, somber and distanced. She wanted to reach out and rescue him from the edge. There was music coming through the PA, a song that had once welcomed both of them back from a shared trip to that edge.

"That's Minmei, isn't it, Rick? Have you two been seeing each other?"

"Sure," he answered flatly. "I watch her on the wall screen, and she sees me in her dreams."

No help in this direction; Lisa apologized.

Rick turned from her and leaned out over the rail.

"She's been spending a lot of time with her cousin Kyle. You know, family comes first."

"Well I'm glad you're all right, Rick. I was worried about you."

That at least brought him around, but there was no change in tone.

"Yeah, I'm feeling great, Lisa. Just great."

She wanted to start from scratch: *Listen, Rick, I'm sorry about Roy, if I can be any help to you—*

"So I hear we've got a new barrier system," he was saying. "And I guess we need it more than ever, right, I mean, since the Council is refusing to allow the civilians to leave—"

"Rick—"

"—and it isn't likely that the Zentraedi are going to call off their attacks."

She let him get it all out and let silence act as a buffer.

"The Council will rescind their order, Rick. The captain says he'll keep the ship right there until they do."

Rick sneered. "Good. And the sooner it happens, the better. I know we're all anxious to get back into battle."

Rick's eyes burned into hers until she could no longer stand it and looked away. Was he blaming her somehow for Roy's death? Had she suddenly been reduced to some malevolent symbol in his eyes? First Lynn-Kyle and his remarks about the military, and now this . . . Below she watched the traffic move along the grid of city streets; she looked long and hard at the Sierra foothills, as if to remind herself that she was indeed back on Earth, back among the living. But even if the Council had a change of heart, even if her father came to his senses and allowed the civilian detainees to disembark, what would become of the SDF-1 and her crew?

Where and when would they find safe haven?

CHAPTER
TWO

LAPSTEIN: In light of the, well, "psychological" problems which beset the Zentraedi after the SDF-1's successful return to Earth, isn't there some justification for suggesting that Khyron should have taken over command of the Imperial Fleet?

EXEDORE (Laughs shortly): We would not be having this interview, of this I can assure you.

LAPSTEIN: Of course... But in terms of strategic impact?

EXEDORE: (After a moment) It could be said that Khyron was more aware of the dangers of cultural contagion than many of us, but he was no longer thinking as a strategist. The SDF-1 was not his main concern; that the ship contained a Protoculture matrix was of little importance. He had by now come to believe that by destroying it he would put an end to what he regarded as a psychic threat to his race. I will leave it to your "psychologists" to examine his underlying motives. But I will add this: He was responding in pure Zentraedi fashion—he recognized potential danger and moved to eliminate it. My hope is that this will rescue his image from what many of your writers have termed "humanness."

Lapstein, *Interviews*

Khyron was possessed by the Invid Flower of Life; without being aware of it, he was by now working against the Zentraedi imperative.

Rawlins, *Zentraedi Triumvirate: Dolza, Breetai, Khyron*

WELL WITHIN STRIKING DISTANCE OF EARTH, two Zentraedi cruisers moved through space, silently, side by side, Gargantuas from an unholy realm. A day would come when the commanders of these ships would stand together at the gates of an even blacker void, released from an artificial past and feverish with exhilaration for a present in the making, hands and hearts linked, an evil pact made good, laughing into the face of death ... But today there were harsh words and recriminations, a taste of what was to come for the rest.

Khyron slammed his fist down on the command post console, his right hand pointed accusingly at the projecbeam image of Azonia, her arms folded across her chest, as much in defiance as in defense.

"It can't be!" the so-called Backstabber shouted. "Why are they ordering us to fall back?"

His lowered head and narrowed eyes peering from beneath bangs of sky blue gave him a demonic look.

Azonia now addressed the projecbeam image on the bridge of her cruiser.

"I'm not at liberty to explain, but our orders are clear, Khyron: Until this new operation is terminated, you will do nothing but stand by and wait. Is that clear?"

She tried to sound calm but knew that he would see through it. Khyron glared at her.

"Don't play games with me, Azonia. That ship grows stronger day by day, while we sit and do nothing."

"Khyron—"

"Your meddling in my plans allowed the Micronians to reach their homeworld. But it is not too late to undo the damage you've done: Destroy them now!"

"Enough!" she screamed at the screen. But he paid her little heed. An angry sweep of dismissal with his arm, bared teeth, and he was gone. The projecbeam compressed to a single horizontal line and vanished, but Azonia tried to raise him nevertheless.

"Khyron, come in, Khyron! Come in at once!"

Too late. She leaned forward to steady herself on stiffened arms, palms still flattened against the com buttons. She knew him well enough to fear him, but it wasn't fear that was threatening to overcome her. These were darker feelings, utterly devoid of light, far worse than fear. And suddenly she recognized what it must be: Commander in Chief Dolza had relieved Breetai of his command, had entrusted her with the mission to retrieve Zor's ship, and she had *failed* him.

Failed him!

Just then Miriya was admitted to the bridge, and Azonia felt a glimmer of hope. If anyone could help her deal with Khyron, it would be Miriya, the Zentraedi's most skilled pilot. But Azonia was soon to learn that Khyron had already undermined these plans also.

"I'm glad that you're here," Azonia said to welcome the female ace. "Commander Khyron is jeopardizing our mission. I'm going to need your help to keep him in line."

Miriya lowered her gaze. "Commander, I . . ."

Azonia approached her with concern. "Miriya, what's wrong? Out with it."

"I have come to request your permission to enter the dimensional fortress . . . as a spy."

Azonia was shocked. "Micronized?!"

"Yes. I have been studying the enemy's language, and I am confident that my presence will profit our cause."

"But why? Why would our finest pilot want to become a Micronian? You're not making sense!"

"Please, Commander, I have no choice."

"Nonsense! Tell me. I order you."

Miriya's deep green eyes flashed; she tossed back her mane of thick hair and glared at Azonia.

"I have been defeated in battle . . . bested by a Micronian, an insignificant *bug*! I must find and destroy that pilot. Until then I'm of use to no one. You must permit me, Commander, for the glory of the Zentraedi."

Defeat! thought Azonia. *Failure! What was to become of their once glorious race?*

Khyron wasted no time putting his attack plan into effect. Moments after breaking contact with Azonia he was on his way to the cruiser's Battlepod hangar, where his lieutenants and squadron leaders would receive their briefing. Every minute lost brought the Zentraedi that much closer to defeat; of this he was certain. The Micronians were making repairs, taking on stores, readying themselves for another round . . .

Defeat . . . There was a time not long ago when the very *word* found no place in his thinking, let alone the idea. But recent events had reshaped his world view; dangerous possibilities were now entertained where none had existed before. This operation directed against the Micronians of "Earth" was beginning to assume portentous dimensions. Left in the dark to puzzle out the intricacies of this war that was not a war, Khyron had been forced to rely on instinct and rumor; he had implicit faith in the former but little use for the latter unless, as in the present case, he found corroborating evidence of his own. And at the center of the complexities was Zor's ship, the Super Dimensional Fortress. That the fortress, with its Protoculture matrix, was a trophy worthy enough to justify the expenditures of this operation was beyond dispute. And that it had to be kept from the Invid, equally so. But surely the Robotech Masters would concede that at this point the fortress was expendable; the Micronians, having already unlocked some of its secrets, posed a threat greater than loss of the ship itself. And threats were best dealt with directly. But what should have been a straightforward eradication and mop-up exercise, no different from scores of similar operations effected throughout the quadrant, had become a hazardous hunt—an attempt to recapture the fortress intact *at any cost*. Had the Commander in Chief forgotten the imperative?

The Zentraedi were a race of warriors, not gamesters.

Just what were Dolza and Breetai up to? Over and over again he put the question to himself. Were they serving the Robotech Masters or some rebellious design of their own? Khyron's suspicions had been temporarily put to rest when Breetai had been relieved of his command, but now he was beginning to consider that this, too, was part of their plan. That Azonia had been chosen to head up the operation was disturbing—maybe a sign that the Old One was in fact losing his grip—but beside the point in any case. Azonia's time had run out; once under way, the present attack plan would accomplish a secondary purpose in seeing to that. But Dolza's next move remained to be seen; should Breetai be returned to command, Khyron would have no choice but to accept his rebellion theory as truth. But he also understood that a schism now would only add to an already perilous course. That was why the present situation had to be defused.

In the cavernous lower chambers of the Zentraedi cruiser, the assault group was assembled. In addition to the usual complement of Botoru tri-thruster assault ships, carapace fighters, and scout recons, there were scores of specialized mecha outfitted with ECM and radar jamming devices. Khyron laid out his simple plan: The dimensional fortress was to be destroyed.

As Khyron prepared to strap into his Officer's Pod assault ship, he exchanged some final words with Grel, who would man the helm in Khyron's absence. The square-jawed face of the First Officer was on the overhead screen in the central hold.

"Wait until I approach the fortress and activate ECM before you follow and land your fleet, Grel."

"Although Earth's atmosphere makes it difficult to maneuver, we will obey."

"See that you do. Intelligence reports indicate that the Micronians care a great deal about their miserable world, so if we bring the fight there, the fortress and the planet will be ours for the taking." Khyron noticed Grel's eyes shift back and forth. "Questions, Grel?"

"No, sir . . . But we are going against Azonia's orders again, aren't we?"

Khyron laughed maliciously. "Just carry out your orders. I'll take care of her after we return."

Khyron lowered the canopy of the Battlepod. He ingested two dried leaves from the Flower of Life and brought his mecha to the edge of the cruiser port.

The first controlled firing of the main gun, the Daedalus *Maneuver, the return to Earth: three "whoopees" in two long years of warfare . . .*

But now there was cause for genuine celebration on the bridge of the dimensional fortress: Gloval's ploy had worked. The North American Ontario Quadrant, one of a growing number of separatist states seeking autonomy from the Council's stranglehold, had agreed to accept the civilians. Ontario had its own reasons for doing so, but the captain wasn't about to ask questions. It felt as though an enormous weight was about to be lifted from his shoulders—he could practically feel the worry lines on his face beginning to fade. Now, if Dr. Lang could only figure some way to transfer Macross City as well, lock, stock, and barrel.

News of the recently received crypto-communication spread like wildfire through the ship. Spontaneous parties were already under way in the streets of the city, and Gloval would have been given a ticker-tape parade if there had been any ticker tape available. Residents were hastily packing and making preparations to leave, embracing one another, sobbing good-byes, taking last looks around. As expected, there were more than a few who wished to remain onboard, but there were to be no exceptions to the captain's orders: All civilians had to go. Perhaps when the war was over, like some "city in flight" the SDF-1 would be taking Earth's children to their destiny...

But most of that was for starry-eyed dreamers and science-fantasy buffs; most of Macross wanted out. The tour was finished; it was time to get back into the real world, reconnect with family left behind, tear up the premature obituaries, and start living again. No more alert sirens waking you up in the middle of a false night, no more military scrip or play money, no asteroid showers, no more—*thank heavens!*—modular transformations. Many of the residents forgot that these same hopes had been dashed only short weeks before.

The Defense Force was never polled as to its feelings, though the results undoubtedly would have proved interesting. To some Macross was the ship's heart, and they had fought hard on Earth and in deep space to protect that transplanted center. To be appointed guardian of their homeworld would have been a fair enough trade-off, but that was not to be the case. The Council had already made this clear: Their orders were to lead the aliens away from Earth, to bring the war back into deep space where it belonged, to act as a decoy until such time as the Earth was suitably prepared to deal with invasion. In other words, they had been singled out for sacrifice. If there was supposed to be some sort of grandiose nobility attached to this, it was not readily apparent. But fortunately for the Council, the Earth, and the dimensional fortress commanders themselves, there were few members of the Defense Force in possession of all the facts.

Rick was belowdecks in the *Prometheus* when Max and Ben brought him the news from the bridge. He was in uniform, number-two torx driver in hand, standing alongside Skull One—Roy Fokker's Veritech. An opened access panel in the nacelle below the cockpit broke the unity of the circular fuselage insignia, but Rick missed the symbolism. Nevertheless, he stared into the exposed circuitry, even tinkered a bit, as if searching for memories of his lost friend. The fighter had been fully repaired and serviced; there were no signs of damage, no evidence of the fatal rounds sustained, but that didn't mean the exorcism had been complete. Roy's presence lingered palpably.

Rick closed the panel as the two corporals approached.

"Just doing some maintenance," Rick said by way of explanation. *Yeah, self-maintenance.*

"I'm not surprised," said Max. "Lisa Hayes told us you were down here."

Ben eyed the fuselage numerals. "Hey, this is Commander Fokker's Skull One, isn't it? I didn't know you were going to be flying it."

"Uh, yeah," Rick answered distantly. "Guess I was lucky to get it as my aircraft assignment."

He turned away from them and put his right hand against the mecha almost reverently. "Nice touch of irony, don't you think? Commander Fokker was always so proud of the fact that he'd never gone down. Now he's... gone, and I get his plane. Me... the guy who's always being shot down—even by our own ordnance. Just kind of ironic, that's all."

Rick's friends exchanged concerned looks, but Max broke out of it and into a smile. He told Rick about the civilians, and the lieutenant said, "Terrific." Undaunted, Max continued.

"Apparently the North American Ontario Quadrant will be accepting them, and the official announcement will be given tomorrow by Captain Gloval."

"So how's about we get a jump on the celebration?" Ben said, full of good humor. "We could hit Macross for some food, drink, whatever else comes along."

"You could use the recreation, Lieutenant," Max hastened to add.

Rick's slow smile was a signal that he'd already made up his mind. He had to get himself out of this funk somehow, and he didn't see how low spirits could stand a chance in Macross just now.

"It sounds good, guys. In fact, it'll be my treat."

Ben beamed. "Well how about that, Max?" He moved between his friends, a head taller than both, draping his arms over their shoulders and leading them away from the Veritech. "Doesn't that sound like something the new pilot of the Skull One would do? C'mon, let's get going before he changes his mind."

Rick glanced over his shoulder at the silent mecha; then he turned his back on it and followed Ben's lead.

Khyron's assault unit launched from the cruiser and plunged into Earth's atmosphere, triple-thrusters brilliant orange against a peaceful field of cloud-studded blue.

The dimensional fortress, still configured like an upright winged techno-knight, was over the city of Toronto when radar alerted the bridge of the impending attack.

Vanessa leaned over her console and tapped in a series of commands. She leaned back in her chair as "paint" and directional symbols began to fill the large screen.

"Multiple radar contacts in five, six, and seven. A fleet of alien spacecraft," she informed the captain. Her words came in a rush. "Pods, recons. Small ships, mostly. Coming in from an altitude of twenty miles, north-northwest."

Gloval didn't want to believe it. "Are you sure?"

"Yes, sir," she answered emphatically.

Sammie moaned, "Oh, no!" as both Lisa and Claudia turned from their forward stations to regard the threat board.

"Just as we were entering the Ontario Quadrant."

"Exactly," said Claudia in a way that meant: *typical!*

Gloval had not moved from the command chair; his hands were tightened on the arms, as much to prevent himself from rising as to get a grip on the situation.

"We cannot afford to come under attack here," he said to the bridge. "Commander Hayes, order all pilots to red alert immediately!"

"Here you are, mister, one giant top sirloin, medium rare," the chef said as he placed cutting board and cut in front of Ben.

He, Max, and Rick were in the Kindest Cut, one of Macross City's finest steak houses. They had elected to sit along the circular counter which ringed the central grills—"close to the action," as Ben put it. Exhaust fans and an enormous copper hood overhead took care of most of the smoke, but you had to be a real red-meat lover to deal with the odors, the sizzle and pop that were inescapable up front.

"Thanks a lot, pal," Ben said, pulling the platter-shaped cutting board toward him.

His friends were staring at the steak in disbelief.

"Does this smell great or what?!" He had knife and fork poised, ready to dig in.

"It sure looks like a lot to eat," Max said tentatively.

A massive hunk of meat was impaled on Ben's fork. "I'm so hungry, I might order another one!" He laughed loudly, then opened his mouth widely, the forkful a scant inch from his mouth, when an announcement blared out over the citywide PA.

"Attention, all fighter pilots: red alert, red alert. This is not a drill . . ."

Max and Rick were already on their feet and heading for the door by the time the message was repeated. Ben, however, was still anchored to his seat, wondering if he had time for just one more bite.

"Hey, Ben, move out!" he heard the lieutenant say.

Ben stood up and contemplated the top sirloin, the small, round potatoes, the heavenly garnish of mushrooms and onions . . .

"Don't move," he told the meal. "I'll be back."

CHAPTER
THREE

And, lo, I saw a winged giant walking among the clouds in the western sky, haloed within a globe of radiant glory, and his body set to gleaming silver in the sun. And tho his hands might be raised in supplication, his heart burned with all the fury of holy fires. And I say unto you that this is the Temple of Mankind, risen and returned to do battle with the forces of evil!

Apocrypha, *The Book of James*

VERITECHS WERE ALREADY BEING MOVED TO THE flight elevators by the time Rick, Ben, and Max reached the hangar of the *Prometheus*. They had their "thinking caps" and harness packs on, likewise their respective red, gold, and blue flight suits. Cat crews and controllers were keeping things orderly; after two years of almost constant fighting, they had the routine down to a T. Lisa's voice was loud and clear through the speakers:

"All fighter squadrons: red alert, red alert. This is not a drill, this is not a drill..."

They wished each other luck, separated, and ran for their individual fighters. Skull One was waiting patiently for Rick, wings back and emblem-emblazoned tailerons folded down. He clambered up into the cockpit and strapped in as he ran a quick status check. He thought of Roy as the canopy descended.

Well, Big Brother, looks like I've been elected to fill your shoes. I'm not looking forward to it. Now, don't get me wrong . . . But piloting your fighter in combat is going to take some getting used to.

Rick was waved forward to the elevator. Once on the flight deck, he spread the mecha's wings and raised the Jolly Roger tailerons while coveralled hookup crews readied the ship for launch. Finally the go signal was given. Rick flashed thumbs up and dropped back against the seat. A fleeting image of Roy Fokker appeared on one of the commo screens.

"Well, ole buddy, this one's for you," Rick said aloud. Then, flipping toggles, he contacted the bridge and added, "This is Skull Leader, and we're movin' out."

The engines were activated, power and sound building. The cat officer dropped, the shooter ducked, and seconds later Skull One was accelerated off the flat-deck's hurricane bow and airborne.

On the bridge of the SDF-1, Claudia turned to Lisa.

"Did he say, 'Skull Leader'?"

"That's right, Claudia." There was almost a note of *pride* in her voice. "Lieutenant Hunter's taking over Commander Fokker's Skull One as of today."

It took Claudia by surprise, but she smiled and turned to the bay, hoping to catch a glimpse of the takeoff.

"Roy would have liked that."

"Skull Leader to Skull wing: I've got bogies on my screen. Estimate fifteen seconds until first contact."

Rick and his men were in a delta formation; below them, also in triplicate, were Indigo and Vermilion, along with several other VT teams. Max and Ben were on the lateral commo screens in Skull One's cockpit.

"Are both of you ready to get the job done?"

"You bet we are, Lieutenant," Ben said.

Max added, "Ready for combat."

Rick felt a reawakened sense of purpose that bordered on sheer exhilaration. It was not the usual prebattle adrenaline rush or any other endorphin high but a settling of the storm that had raged inside him since the ship's return to Earth and had peaked with Roy's death —a storm that had whipped him into a frenzy and left him depleted of spirit, faith, the very will to go on. But now, out in this wild blue yonder, those storm clouds were breaking up, and with them that ominous sense of doom and impenetrable darkness. Skull One was airborne again; Rick Hunter was airborne again. Where before he had seen irony, he now felt a curious but calming harmony. He would prevail!

In the lead ship of the alien assault group, Khyron was thinking the same thing. But where Rick's thoughts were tuned to life, Khyron's were attuned to death—as

clear an example as any of the differences that separated
Human from Zentraedi.

"They're dead ahead," Khyron said to his pilots.
"Keep your shields up and fire when ready. Let's get
them now!"

So saying, he engaged the ship's boosters, signaling
his wingmen to follow suit, and threw his forces against
Hunter's.

The two groups met head-on, filling the skies with
thunder. Explosions bloomed and erupted like some
hellish aeroponic garden. Brilliant blue and yellow
tracers crisscrossed with contrails and the smoke and
fire falls of destroyed ships. Wingmen broke away from
their leaders to engage the enemy mecha one on one in
an aerial free-for-all. VT pilots sometimes used the anal-
ogy of boxing versus street fighting: There were no rules;
your opponent was unskilled but mean-spirited and more
than likely unstoppable.

Zentraedi snub-nosed tri-thrusters, triple-finned and
resembling stylized faucet controls, tore through the
Veritech formations, plastron cannons blazing, blue fire
holing craft and pilots alike. Twin top-mounted rockets
were elevated to firing positions, launched, and more
often than not found their mark, throwing fiery debris
into the arena; balls of flame that were once Veritechs
plunged from the sky.

But the Robotech forces hit back.

Skull One banked sharply to avoid the debris of an
exploded craft, angry blue fire deep within its aft thrust-

ers, red-tipped pyloned heat-seekers eager for release. Rick trimmed his ship only to find that he had four more bandits on his tail. He led them on a merry chase, up into a booster climb to the edge of night, then down in a power dive they hadn't anticipated.

Rick threw down the G lever and thought the mecha through to Guardian configuration. He flew into the face of his pursuers like a bird of prey, taloned legs engaged and rear undercarriage guns erupting when he'd cleared their formation. Orange fire blazed from beneath the wings.

A Zentraedi ship exploded, then a second, as it kamikazeed in on Skull One, an expanding cloud of orange death. *Divine wind*, *indeed*, thought Rick.

The Guardian was hovering now, utilizing the downward-pointing foot thrusters for loft and stability and pouring out fire against the two remaining ships. And once again, Rick's thoughts and shots found their mark.

He heard Ben's voice above the racket on the tac net.

"Hey, Skull Leader, that was mighty fine flying, but you've got to be more careful!"

But it was Ben who wasn't being careful: An enemy mecha had him locked on target and was about to open up. Fortunately, Max Sterling had been monitoring the approach; he had the craft lined up in his reticle, and he loosed two rockets to take it out.

Rick heard Ben's cry of surprise, then delight, as Max brought his blue-trimmed ship alongside Dixon's port wingtip.

"You okay, Ben?" Max asked, a lilt to his voice.

"Yeah, sure, now I am, thanks."

"Well, stay alert, big guy."

"Better believe it. Nobody tunes out Ben Dixon!"

Rick was too involved in the battle to notice that several alien ships had peeled away from the attack group and established a holding pattern not far from the SDF-1. This did not go unnoticed on the bridge of the fortress itself, however, or onboard the cruiser commanded by Khyron's second, Grel.

Grel, arms folded across his chest, studied the blue projecbeam field. Deep within a schematic representation of the planetary rim, a bright red light bar flashed once, then twice more. And over the com came the voice of one of the fleet commanders.

"Sir, the radar-jamming tactic appears to be working. Shall we now proceed?"

Grel leaned forward over the console. "Yes, proceed as planned."

As he gave the word, five enormous warships began a slow descent toward Earth.

Gloval stood at the forward bay of the bridge, white cap pulled low on his head, eyes heavy with concern. In the western sky flashes of devilish fire marked the battle zone, discs and crescents in the dusk. South, a cluster of enemy craft in a curious holding pattern, and below the fortress, a city in chaos—a city in peril. What were the residents to make of these unannounced fireworks? Gloval wondered. The SDF-1 was headed north at a good clip, but would it clear these population centers before the battle escalated? He knew it would. He closed his eyes to shut out the scene. He had brought the fortress here to disembark the civilians, and in so doing he had endangered yet another group. Was there no winning this thing—on any front?

"Sir, radar is destabilizing."

Gloval didn't bother to turn and face Vanessa; wearily, he said, "The Zentraedi are jamming our signal... One thing after another... Alert Skull Team to begin a recon sweep of the area." Then he swung around. "Put the new barrier system on standby and be prepared for new enemy activity."

Claudia exercised her prerogative by pointing out that activating the shields would draw power from the weaponry systems, but the captain was way ahead of her; he had little patience left for ground already covered. "I understand the problem, but I must consider the safety of *all* personnel aboard. Now, put the new system on standby immediately!"

"Yes, sir," Claudia deferred. "Stand by to engage..."

Meanwhile, a solitary ship of bizarre design was on a low, silent approach to the dimensional fortress, taking advantage of a ridge of low hills to conceal itself from detection and involvement in the raging battle. The mecha was insectlike in appearance, with a globular twin-hemisphered body, pincer arms, two cloven legs, and a pointed proboscis cockpit module. It was not a Botoru ship—one of Khyron's Seventh Mechanical Division—but a Quadrono. And held in the grip of the armored right hand, contained in a transparent chamber similar to that which had delivered three micronized spies into the SDF-1, was the female ace of that fleet, Miriya Parino. She wore a sleeveless blue-gray sackcloth of a dress, belted with rough cord, and carried no weapons.

It was this last that worried the female pilot of the mecha. She had visual contact with Miriya via the curved screen in the cockpit, audio through the helmet communicator.

"Miriya, this is dangerous! Are you certain you want to board the Micronian ship with no weapons?"

"I won't need weapons."

"But Commander Azonia is already upset about the failure of this operation . . ."

"Upset, but not with me. It's Khyron who has made a mess of things." *And some of us are aware of the* special *rivalries that exist between Azonia and Khyron*, she wanted to add. But Miriya had no quarrel with the Backstabber. He was now doubly responsible for her mission and her present micronized size: first by alerting her to the Micronian ace who had bested her in battle, and second by launching yet another unauthorized attack against the SDF-1. The battle had simplified the infiltration considerably. But these facts were of no use to the pilot.

"Just deliver me to the Micronian ship," Miriya said sternly.

* * *

Khyron had removed himself from the aerial arena; his command mecha was positioned at the southern perimeter of the skirmish, and he had managed to raise Grel on the com. The lieutenant's face appeared on a secondary commo screen in the cockpit while explosive flashes of battle light strobed against the outer hull of the ship.

"We're hovering above the surface, awaiting your further orders, my lord."

Khyron was pleased enough to compliment his second.

"Excellent, Grel, you've done a superb job. Now, prepare your attack, but don't open fire until I join you."

"My lord!" Grel saluted.

Following Gloval's orders, Skull Team had also temporarily absented themselves from the battle to recon south of the fortress. Rick had patched the infrared scanners, wide and long-range, into the commo system; center and lateral screens now afforded him an image-enhanced sweep of the horizon. In a moment he had radar contact and upped the magnification on the screens. Gloval was right: Zentraedi cruisers!

Rick activated the scrambler and went on the tac net.

"Lisa, are you monitoring?"

She answered, "Affirmative," from the bridge and notified the captain: "Skull has visuals on five alien cruisers; range, seventy miles, south-southeast, vector headings coming in now..."

"All right," said Gloval, hands behind his back at the

forward bay. "Claudia, activate the omnidirectional barrier at once!"

In the new shield system control room, more than a dozen techs and specialists readied themselves. Situated aft and well below the bridge in a huge hold, the room itself was little more than a flyout platform equipped with a central readout table and numerous manned consoles and viewscreens. But the device responsible for the energy barrier was something else again. Blue rings of pulsed energy filled the hold as Gloval gave word to engage the system. Power began to build in the field generator—an enormous gearlike dish with eight hydraulic closure teeth—while its mate telescoped down on a thick shaft from the hold overhead. Short of meshing, the generators exchanged phrases of fire, forming and containing a sphere of effulgent energy.

On the bridge the energy sphere registered schematically on Claudia's console monitor as a globe-shaped grid fully encompassing the upright SDF-1.

Externalized, the sphere was a yellow-green cloud that grew and expanded from the ship's center, gaseous and slightly luminescent, haloing the fortress in the night sky.

Grel was viewing its formation on the command center screen as Khyron entered, his harness pack and hip blasters still in place.

"What's going on?" he demanded.

Grel didn't bother to salute. "There's a large energy shield surrounding the Micronian ship."

Khyron snorted. "I don't care. Open fire, now!"

* * *

It was as if someone had scribbled across the sky with a light crayon . . . that many rockets were launched from the Zentraedi warships. Ninety-eight percent of them found their mark, enveloping and obscuring the dimensional fortress in a minute-long symphony of explosions. But to the amazement of human and Zentraedi alike the shield absorbed the deadly storm, and the fortress was left unscathed.

"It's unlike anything we've encountered," said Grel, commenting on a profile schematic of the Micronian shield. "And it seems to be fully protecting the ship from our attack. So what now?"

"Yes . . ." Khyron answered slowly. "Advance the group and continue firing until I order you to cease."

And continue they did, employing pulsed lasers and cannon fire. Streaks of horizontal lightning converged on the SDF-1, but to no avail. What the shield didn't absorb, it simply deflected.

Captain Gloval was cautiously optimistic; the barrier system was holding, but Vanessa's threat board showed that the enemy had advanced well into the yellow zone.

"The enemy is continuing their attack," she warned him.

His hopes dashed, the captain gave voice to his fears.

"This time they won't stop coming until they've destroyed us."

Sammie turned her frightened eyes to him. "Sir, couldn't we radio headquarters and ask for some support or something?"

"That won't work," Lisa chided her. "The captain knows a request like that would just be ignored."

"Because we've been making so many demands about the civilians?" Kim asked.

It was the wrong time for foolish questions, but Gloval fielded them patiently. "It has more to do with our proximity to the ground," he told her. He'd placed his own head on the chopping block; it was unlikely that anyone in the Council would come to his rescue.

"Message, sir."

Gloval turned his attention to Claudia's overhead monitor. It was one of Lang's Robotechnicians.

"We've got a serious problem, Captain. The barrier system is beginning to overload!"

Rick and the members of Skull Team had been watching the bombardment in awe, but Lisa was now ordering them to counterattack the warships.

"You've got to draw their fire, Lieutenant Hunter. The shields can't take any more. If you fail . . .

"There isn't going to be any ship to return to."

Her eyes shifted on the screen, as if trying to find his across miles of sky. "It looks bad, Rick. Captain Gloval wants you to know that as of this moment, the safety of every single person on this ship rests in your hands."

The safety of every single person on this ship rests in your hands . . . Bottom of the ninth: bases loaded, two outs, Hunter on deck . . .

Skull Team descended on the cruisers like vengeful eagles. They had reconfigured to Guardian mode for the drop and to Battloid now as they touched down on the first warship, skimming over its armored green hull, blue foot thrusters blazing like power skaters. Gatlings resounding, they moved toward the stern, taking out turret guns and sealing weapons ports. But that still left four ships emitting unbroken lines of blue death.

The once clearly defined schematic sphere was now a vaguely circular blotch bleeding sickly colors across the Zentraedi projecbeam field.

"You see," Grel said knowingly, "their energy readings are dropping quickly. The shield is at its limit."

Khyron laughed through his teeth. "Now these Micronians will be mine. *Mine!*"

Inside the SDF-1 the barrier system generators lost their grip on that shared and maintained globe of energy; the ball flattened, grew savagely oblate, then lost its circumference entirely and began to arc untamed throughout the hold.

The bridge was in chaos.

"Barrier generators four and seven are losing power due to intense core overheating," Claudia reported to Gloval. Her monitor schematic revealed weakened coordinates along the shield grid.

The captain quickly ordered her to switch to subsystem power.

Meanwhile three of the nine screens at Kim's station and two at Sammie's had blacked out; two others were flashing a field of orange static.

"We have an overload situation in the outer field circuits ..."

"Number seven converter has exceeded its limit ..."

"Emergency backup crew, report to your service areas."

Lisa brought her hands to her ears and went on the aircom net. "Skull Leader, keep your comline open for emergency orders."

The threat board showed the Zentraedi warships continuing their advance. "They've just entered the red zone, Captain!" Vanessa shouted.

Then, suddenly, there was a blood-curdling scream through the patch lines from the shield control room and primary lighting failed. The bridge crew looked like the living dead under the eerie glow of console lights. Klaxons and warning sirens were blaring from remote areas of the fortress. Sammie's station screen had gone fully to orange.

"It's reaching critical mass," she yelled. "It's going to explode!"

Rick heard the panic in Lisa's voice. "Skull Leader, evacuate your team at once—the barrier system is about to chain-react. Evacuate—"

Rick, Max, and Ben thought their Battloids through an about-face. Beyond the rim of the Zentraedi warship they could see the barrier transubstantiate: What appeared as the selfsame shield was in fact shot through and through with submolecular death.

Rick watched as radiation detector gauges came to

life in the cockpit. He raised his teammates on the tac net and told them to clear out on the double

Behind them the shield expanded, its internal colors shifting from green through yellow and orange to deadly red; then, after a blinding flash of silent white light, the shield was gone. In its place a hot pink hemisphere began to form, an umbrella of horror fifty miles wide.

The three pilots ran their Battloids along the armored hull, past turrets and singed bristle sensors already slagging in the infernal heat; they reconfigured to Guardian mode and launched themselves, the spreading shock wave threatening to overtake them.

Rick glimpsed one of the warships rise from the pack and accelerate itself to safety. But the rest were annihilated, atomized along with every standing structure and living thing on the ground.

Skull One was tearing through fuchsia skies, fire nipping at the fighter's tail. Inside, Rick searched desperately right and left for a sign of his wingmen. Max's ship came into view to port, but Ben was nowhere in sight.

"Ben, Ben!" Rick cried.

"Behind you, Lieutenant!"

Rick found Dixon's radar blip on the screen; Ben was converting to Guardian for added thrust.

"Hit your afterburner—now! Do you copy?"

Ben's voice was terror-filled: "It's too late, Rick! I can't make . . . Aaarrrggghhh! . . ."

Rick shook his head wildly, as much to deny the truth as to keep the sound of death from his ears.

He crossed himself as Ben's radar image began to fade.

A second friend lost...color gone out of the world...

CHAPTER
FOUR

All of a sudden it seemed everything was out of control. Here we were back on Earth, feeling more displaced than we'd felt in deep space. The Council refused to hear us out. The Zentraedi attacks continued unabated, we'd lost Roy Fokker and Ben Dixon, and thousands of innocents had been killed. I wasn't alone in feeling this sense of hopelessness. But it was something we weren't supposed to discuss, as though we had all agreed to some unspoken rule: By not talking about it we could make it go away . . . Day by day it was becoming more difficult for us to find any sense of comfort or acceptance in Macross, and here was Lynn-Kyle adding fuel to the fire, spearheading a peace movement which could only further undermine our attempts to defeat the aliens. Not that there wasn't ample justification for civil unrest. But we were one ship, one cause—no thanks to Russo's Council—an independent nation at war with the Zentraedi! I had personal reasons for disliking [Kyle], but I now found reasons to distrust him as well. That he had turned Minmei against me, I accepted as given. But I couldn't stand still and allow him to threaten the ship, that military/civilian integrity essential for our survival.

The Collected Journals of Admiral Rick Hunter

THE ENEMY ENERGY POURED INTO AND ABSORBED BY the barrier cloud had chain-reacted; at the center of the ensuing explosion the SDF-1 was left relatively untouched, but on the ground countless thousands were dead. Within a twenty-five-mile radius from the fortress the Earth's surface was scorched and flayed beyond recognition.

As a consequence, the Ontario Quadrant subcommand had refused to allow the SDF-1 civilians to disembark; those onboard who had heard the rumors early on ceased their premature celebrations and faced the heartbreak.

Eight of the twenty-one techs who manned the barrier system controls had been killed, and the rest were listed in critical condition. The air corps had suffered heavy casualties.

Ben Dixon had tuned out...

But the really big news in Macross City focused on Lynn-Minmei: She had been hospitalized for exhaustion.

Reporters caught up with Lynn-Kyle on the steps of Macross General. The long-haired star was angry enough to create a scene, but he thought better of it and decided to use the news coverage to his advantage. He left their rapid questions unanswered until they got the hint and backed off to let him speak.

"What does Minmei's doctor say?"

"What is the prognosis?"

"Kyle, how long will she be hospitalized?"

"Come on, give us *something*—you're her closest friend."

"How is this going to affect the shooting schedule for the movie the two of you are doing?"

"All right, listen up," Kyle said at last. "I want to make a statement concerning the war. In the midst of all that's going on, all this continual destruction and loss of life, you people want to ask me about Minmei's health. Are you all blind to the realities of this situation or what?"

One of the reporters smirked. "I get it, we should be focusing on *your* needs, huh?"

Kyle shot him an angry look. "Have you ever stopped to consider the priorities? You're prisoners aboard this ship, we're still under attack, the Council has written you all off, you're being lied to left and right, and you spend your time chasing after a celebrity who's fainted from overwork! Forget this nonsense. We've got to find a way to put an end to this war."

"What would you have everyone do, Kyle?"

"Are you planning to head up a new peace movement?"

"Open rebellion, passive resistance, letters to Command—what are you advocating?"

Kyle held up his hands, then pointed toward one of the group as he responded. "It's *your* responsibility to expose these cover-ups. Point out the lies and contradictions. Show the people of this city the military leaders *as they really are*. We've got to begin pressuring them. We're fifty thousand strong, and we *can* put a stop to this.

"Right now all we've got is devastation and destruction—no winners, only losers. This is an inhumane, no-win situation. The only *conquest* that should concern us is the conquest of our warring nature."

Kyle V-ed the fingers of his right hand and held it aloft.

"*Peace* must conquer all!"

While Lynn-Kyle was urging the press to smoke out enemies of peace from Senator Russo's Council and the SDF-1's leadership command, Earth's fate was under discussion several billion miles away. Khyron's cruiser, the lone survivor of the barrier shield chain-reaction explosion, had refolded to Dolza's command fortress with trans-vids of the catastrophic event. The Zentraedi Commander in Chief was viewing these now, shock and deep concern on his ancient stone face. Breetai, on the other hand, wore a self-satisfied, knowing grin.

Wide-eyed, Dolza ordered a replay of the video—a second look at that enormous canopy of destruction, that hemispheric rain of death, a hapless Micronian city atomized, a verdant land utterly denuded.

"These Micronians are more ruthless than I first believed," the Old One was willing to admit. "They were prepared to sacrifice an entire population center simply to defeat four small divisions of attacking mecha!" Without turning to Breetai, he added, "I suppose their determination comes as no surprise to you, Commander."

Breetai swung around to face Dolza, his grin of self-vindication still in place. He placed one arm on the table and said simply, "No, sir."

"Commander Azonia's inexperience with these beings

has proved to be an obvious liability. I am therefore sending you back to take charge of our forces."

Breetai narrowed his eyes at the pronouncement; he'd anticipated this moment for some time. "On one condition," he told Dolza, taking delight in the Old One's disgruntled reaction. "I must request that the Imperial Fleet be redeployed and placed under my command."

"Why such a large force?" Dolza demanded.

Breetai gestured to the wall screen. "You have seen what the Micronians are capable of. They are unpredictable and dangerous. I'm going to need the extra resources."

"Very well, then. You have them," Dolza said stiffly.

Breetai rose and brought his right fist to his left breast in salute. "Your lordship."

Dismissed, he started for the door, but Dolza called out to him, "One more thing, *Commander*."

Neither one of them turned around: Dolza sat stonefaced in his chair; Breetai stood straight and unmoving, right hand clenched at his side. He glanced back over his shoulder.

"I expect you to give me better results this time."

The words dripped with menace, the implication clear.

"You'll not be disappointed with my performance, m'lord."

When Breetai reached the sliding door, Dolza added, "For your sake, I hope not."

Exedore was waiting for him in the corridor, eager to learn the results of the brief meeting. Breetai brought his adviser up to date as they returned to the flagship. The first stage of the journey—one that suitably suggested the enormous size of the command center—was on foot. The two Zentraedi walked for several minutes until they reached an egress port, where a curved platform jutted out into the command center's central chamber. This was a vast low-g space of water-vapor clouds and what might have appeared to human eyes as blue skies. An open-aired-hover-dish met them at the edge of the railed flyout and transferred them to a waiting shuttle, one of several "anchored" in antigrav stasis. In true Zentraedi fashion, these shuttlecraft resembled nothing more than oddly shaped fish, with two small circular "mouths," one above the other at the ship's snout, and ventral forehead slits and bilateral gill membranes aft, which were actually the exterior drive housings. The shuttlecraft conveyed them through the heart of the chamber—over a veritable city given over to the Robotechnological devices which maintained the command center—to the main docking area where ships-of-the-line, cruisers, destroyers, and battlewagons were anchored. Ultimately they were delivered into the flagship itself. Breetai insisted that they go directly to the bridge.

The observation bubble which overlooked astrogation and the command post's circular viewscreen were in ruins, unchanged since Max Sterling had piloted a VT through them over two months before. But at least the debris had been carted away and the commander's chair and twin microphonelike communicators were intact.

"I'll be most eager to hear what our spies have to report when they return from their mission," Breetai was saying.

"Yes, our emergence from hyperspace will be the signal they've been waiting for." Exedore continued, "Their observations should prove most enlightening, my lord. Surely we'll learn to what extent the Micronians have applied their knowledge of Protoculture. From there it should prove a simple step to redesign our offensive campaign."

"Let us hope so, Exedore," Breetai said noncommittally. "Now, give the order to all vessels of the Imperial Fleet to prepare for an immediate fold operation."

Exedore turned to his task. Klaxons were soon sounding, and announcements were issued from the PA.

"All vessels move to fold position . . . Axis pattern adjust to flagship's attitude . . . countdown has begun . . . Hyperspace-fold to commence in exactly one minute . . ."

Exedore surveyed the vessels of the Imperial Fleet as the countdown sounded. He was pleased with Breetai's reawakened confidence. But there was something . . . some nagging doubt remained at the edge of his thoughts. Words of warning from the ancient texts continued to erode his strength. A secret weapon, *a secret weapon* . . .

One million warships readied themselves for the fold.

And Exedore wondered: *Will they be enough?*

* * *

On the way to his quarters in Barracks C, Rick heard his name being paged and walked over to one of the yellow courtesy phones.

Minmei.

"Rick, I'm so glad I got you. I guess you've heard the news that I passed out. Well, it's true. I'm in the hospital now, but I don't want you to worry about me. It was just overwork, and now I'm catching up on some much-needed rest . . . Oh, Rick, why don't you come over and visit me. It would be great; I could really use the company. You don't have to bring me anything—"

He replaced the handset in its cradle, stood there staring at it for a moment, uncertain, then walked off. Again he heard his name paged, but this time he ignored it.

He went straight to the computer keyboard in his quarters, sat down, and began to hammer away at the keys methodically and without pause. He commanded the printer on-line and tore free the single sheet he'd completed.

"Dear Mr. and Mrs. Dixon," he read aloud. "As your son's commanding officer, it is my sad duty to inform you that—"

Ben, hit your afterburners—now!

Rick crumpled the paper in his hands and threw it aside in anger. "I just can't do it!" he shouted to the monitor.

Beside him on the desk was a photo of Ben and his parents taken years ago, along with a letter from them that had arrived too late. Rick took hold of them and stood up.

They were both so proud of him! There's nothing I can say to make this any easier. It seems like such a waste!

There was a knock at the door; he replaced the items and went to answer it, a weary stranger in his own room.

At the door it all caught up with him. Palms pressed against the cool metal for support, he stood there and sobbed, letting his pain wash out uncontrolled. Then suddenly he spun round at the sound of a familiar voice, a ghostly hallucination his mind wanted desperately to embrace.

Ben was leaning over the computer, as though reading what Rick had written, one foot crossed in front of the other, his characteristic grin in place.

Lieutenant, old buddy—hi! . . . Hey, I know you're feelin' bad, but it couldn't be helped. It was just my time to go.

Rick turned away from the apparition, complimenting one part of himself for a nice try. But he wasn't about to let himself off the hook that easily.

He hid his face and tears from Max as the door slid open. Sterling spied the photo and letter but said nothing. He reminded Rick that the two of them were due on deck shortly, and they left the room together a minute later.

Why wasn't Max equally broken up about Ben's death? Rick asked himself. What was it his mind had materialized only moments before to bring him peace or resignation: *It couldn't be helped, it was just my time to go* . . . Was there something to that?

In the elevator Max seemed to read his thoughts.

"I guess it's tough being in command," he told Rick. "I mean, after a while you start feeling responsible for everybody who's serving under you, right?"

Rick turned on him. "You don't know how helpless I feel each time we go into battle. Each time we . . . *lose* someone. It's like letting someone slip from your grasp and fall. You're always wondering if there wasn't something more you could have done, something you overlooked."

"I wonder if I'll feel that way when I get *my* first command."

Max's response surprised him; he wasn't going to get the sympathy he'd expected.

"It's probably coming soon," Max continued. "Command just promoted me to second lieutenant, and it's barely a month since I was promoted to third lieutenant."

They were ascending the wide staircase that led to the starboard observation deck overlooking the *Daedalus*. Rick stopped to look at Max.

"I'm sure you'll make a good commander."

Rick's tone was flat, but he meant it; Max not only had the required skills, he had the faith and will to carry on—he knew how to stow away the horrors. Rick thought he'd achieved that after Roy's death. Before the battle he had felt renewed, but with Ben's death that feeling had faded. In its place was a hopelessness he could barely bring himself to confront.

A female tower controller's voice rang out over the ob deck speakers: "Unloading will commence in exactly one minute. Please be sure all cargo bay doors are open to receive supply consignments from helicopter shuttle groups. Under flight decks should now be clear and convoy vehicles in place to continue transfer to warehouse distribution centers..."

The SDF-1 was back at its original landing site in the Pacific, floating now in Cruiser mode like some techno-island. For days, huge cargo carriers and choppers had been flying in all make and manner of supplies and provisions. Trucks and transports lumbered through the streets of Macross city day and night, confirming the worst fears of the civilians aboard: The battle fortress was no longer welcome on Earth.

Max pointed out a fancy-looking double-bubbled jet chopper coming out of pink and lavender sunset clouds to set down on the carrier deck. In addition to the Robotech insignia, it bore black and gold Earth Council markings.

"Gotta be somebody important," Max guessed.

"It's from Alaska HQ. I'll bet they brought lift-off orders. We're the only thing standing between Earth and the Zentraedi, but they're ready to toss us to the sharks, anyway."

Following Rick's lead, Max put his elbows on the rail and leaned over for a better look at the chopper.

"You think it's true about us being banished from Earth?"

Rick nodded and straightened up. "They've pulled in the welcome mat. This ship is going to be our home for a long time to come."

"Then this might be the last time we get to see the Earth from the surface," Max mused. "Guess we'd better enjoy the view."

The sun was setting over planet Earth. Rick stared into the orb's orange glow; there was a finality to the moment too frightening to contemplate.

She was an attractive woman with pleasant features and a crop of long brown hair, but she carried herself stiffly and kept her officer's cap pulled too low on her forehead. Besides, she had brought bad news.

She turned around in the doorway to Gloval's quarters and saluted. "I'll let headquarters know the orders were received." Two white-jacketed, blue-capped aides, brass buckles of their belts gleaming, registered looks of distaste and followed her down the corridor.

The captain remained seated at the desk in his spacious quarters. A Defense Forces flag stood to one side of the desk in an area partitioned off by a tall bookcase and dominated by a large wall screen. Insignia carpets, bright throw rugs, and potted plants warmed the room; the leatherbound volumes and computer consoles lent just the right air of officiality.

Gloval had the orders in hand. He lighted his pipe and

leaned in to read through them. *Yes*, he said to himself, thinking about the female officer, *the orders have been received*. And she could tell those idiot generals back at headquarters that they were received in silence, *completely under protest*.

It was unthinkable—expected but unbelievable nonetheless. The Council didn't have an ounce of pity in their hearts.

Gloval got up and paced, then returned to the desk.

What was he supposed to say to the people of the ship?

Silently, he read: *The United Earth Council hereby orders that you remove the dimensional fortress from any close proximity to the Earth. You are also ordered to detain until such time as this governing Council sees fit all civilian refugees onboard. Should you fail to carry out these orders to the letter, this Council will recommend to the Joint Chiefs of Staff—*

Gloval threw the papers aside in disgust. He responded to a knock on the door and bade Lisa enter. She picked up the note of anger and frustration in his voice and asked if there was anything wrong.

Gloval had his back to her, smoke rising from his pipe like steam from an ancient locomotive. "Yes, there's something wrong—as wrong as can be." He gave her a sidelong glance. "But it's just as we feared: We've been ordered to leave Earth immediately."

Gloval heard her sharp intake of breath, but she rallied quickly and offered to fix him a drink. She was a trooper all right.

"After the explosion I expected the ship to be exiled. But to force fifty thousand innocent civilians to become refugees from their own planet—

Lisa handed him a Scotch on the rocks; she had fixed herself one as well.

"I guess we should drink a toast to our last moments on Earth, Lisa."

"Perhaps we should drink a toast to the civilians instead."

It seemed an appropriate gesture; they raised their glasses and took long pulls of the expensive stuff.

"These orders go into effect as soon as we've finished taking on supplies. That means we'll be forced to break the news of our banishment to everyone just moments before we take off."

"Do you want me to announce it?" Lisa volunteered.

"No, I'd better make the broadcast myself."

Lisa left to make the necessary arrangements. Gloval dropped down into his chair, took a deep breath, and punched in the bridge on his phone. Claudia informed him that loading was almost complete.

"Now, listen to me carefully, Claudia," he began. Sweat was even now beading up on his forehead; how would it be when he went out in front of the entire ship? "I want you to quietly begin preparations to move out."

"To where, Captain?"

"I'll have astrogation furnish you with the coordinates immediately. You see, we're leaving Earth."

CHAPTER
FIVE

> *It is no secret (nor should it come as any surprise) that humankind's most noble impulses often surface during the most trying of times, that human spirit rises to the challenge when faced with adversity, that human strength is born from human failings ... Is it any wonder, then, that the SDF-1 crew became a tighter family after the fortress had been exiled than it had been before?*

From the log of Captain (later Admiral) Henry Gloval

IN THEIR DARK AND DANK HIDEOUT DEEP WITHIN THE bowels of the dimensional fortress, the three Zentraedi spies sat down to their last Micronian meal; soon they would attempt an escape that would end either in their deaths or in a successful rendezvous with the ships of the main fleet. The three—Rico, Konda, and Bron— agreed that their mission would have been judged superlative had they only been able to leave the fortress to reconnoiter the Micronian homeworld; but oddly enough, few of the Micronians had been allowed to disembark. Nevertheless they were pleased with what they had managed to amass over the course of the past three months by Micronian reckoning. The operational Battlepod which they had been lucky enough to obtain was ready for flight, crowded now with the results of their many forays into Macross City in search of espionage booty, Micronian artifacts, and, well, *souvenirs*— two video monitors, a few tables, a refrigerator, a grand piano they had smuggled home in pieces, disc players and discs, candy and foodstuffs, and, of course, a wide assortment of Minmei dolls and paraphernalia.

Bron, as always, had prepared the meal.

"Something called beef stew," he explained.

"Smells terrific," said Konda, purple hair now below his shoulders.

Metal plates and bent silverware in hand, the three agents, looking unwashed and shaggy, their clothing soiled and threadbare, were seated on short lengths of cowling and empty cans around a blazing liquid-fueled camping stove, currently crowned by a large, lidded stew pot. Rico had switched on the portable CD player; Minmei's "Stagefright" was filling the little-used storage room with pleasing sounds.

Rico put aside the device that would alert them to the rearrival of the Zentraedi fleet and said, "Listening to Minmei helps my food go down better."

"She makes *everything* better," Konda seconded.

Their spirits were high, ebullient; even Bron, who managed to burn his hands while removing the stew pot from the flame. As always. He placed a coffeepot on the stove and sampled a bit of the day's fare.

"What about my cooking, boys—do you think it's improved some?"

"Yeah," said Konda, straight-faced, "it takes me over an hour to get indigestion now."

Bron's response was equally low-key. "That *is* better. It used to take you fifteen minutes."

"When he first started cooking, *I* used to get sick just *thinking* about it!"

Rico broke up, and his comrades joined in. The coffee, meanwhile, was boiling away, running down the sides of the pot and adding sizzle to the fire.

But Bron grew serious all of a sudden. "To be honest, I'm going to miss this Micronian food."

The subject broached, other disclosures followed.

"Well, I hate to admit it, but you're right—me, too."

"And that's not all. I've been thinking, I'm gonna miss a whole lotta things—like happy people, music—"

"Yeah, the music. The thing I'll miss most is hearing Minmei sing every day."

The corners of Bron's mouth turned down. "I don't even want to *think* about that."

"And you remember those females we met that one time?" Konda poured himself a cup of coffee. "Dancing was fun."

"Yeah, that Kim was really something else," said Bron, the enthusiasm returned. "She had me laughing almost all day!"

"And that girl Sammie," Rico was quick to add, hand

to his face demonstrating a Micronian gesture he'd observed. "When she spotted us with the Minmei doll . . . 'My heavens!'" He mimicked Sammie's voice.

They shared a good laugh, but again the mood deteriorated.

"Yeah . . . And you remember what we heard that Micronian talking about—about trying to put an end to the war?"

"That frightened me," said Rico. "Without war we'd have no reason to live!"

"Maybe," Konda answered him. "But I kinda feel like I understand what the Micronian was talkin' about."

Rico reached out and touched the gravity-wave indicator beside him on the floor. "It's hard to believe that by tomorrow morning we'll all probably be back in uniform."

"Yeah . . ."

"I can hardly wait . . ."

Claudia Grant also found herself breaking out in a cold sweat as she relayed the captain's orders to the bridge crew.

"Takeoff?" said Vanessa. "You mean to say all those rumors about leaving are true?"

"Let's be realistic. We caused an entire city to be wiped out." Kim's hand was at her mouth, as though trying to stifle the truth.

Sammie looked over from her station innocently. "We weren't responsible—it was the barrier overload. Blame it on the Zentraedi."

"But we shouldn't have been there," Kim argued.

"The captain was thinking of the civilians, Kim—"

"What's going to happen to them?" Vanessa broke in.

Claudia was on tiptoes, throwing switches to activate the overhead monitors at her and Lisa's stations. She turned around, a hint of impatience in her voice. "Since they've already been declared dead and nobody on Earth wants to accept them, I guess they'll stay with us. Now, hurry up with those final checks; we're running out of time."

Sammie struck a daydreamer's pose at her console. "Lisa's father is a bigshot in the United Earth Council. Maybe if she sent him a message, he'd hold up our orders until we figured out—Oh—"

Claudia, hands on hips, was standing over her.

"Don't you *think* about suggesting that to Lisa, do you understand? As an officer aboard this ship, she knows her duties. Now, see to it that you carry out yours!"

Lovers watching the skies that night thought they were viewing an unannounced solar eclipse. The full moon wore a diamond ring of brilliant light. But wait... *an unannounced solar eclipse?* The sun had set over four hours ago!

Amateur astronomers were similarly puzzled, as were seismologists and sailors; graphs and gauges were going wild, and Earth's oceans were rising to dangerous heights... But there were a few scientists scattered across the planet who recognized the phenomenon;

they'd witnessed these gravity-wave disturbances once before, a little over two years ago. But where that initial event had brought awe, the present event brought terror.

To three beings on the planet, however, the event was little more than a signal.

"That's it!" said Bron, deactivating the transceiver. "Let's move out!"

The agents were already inside the Battlepod, strapped in and alert. They ran the pod ostrichlike across the hold, metal hooves loud against the floorplates, echoes granting them an illusory sense of company, stopping a few feet short of the exterior hull. Bursts from the mecha's twin lasers concentrated blue-white energy on the hull. The steel glowed red, then white, slagged, and began to fall away; flames leapt forth, and the small hole enlarged. Within minutes there was an enormous breach, large enough to accommodate the pod's passage into the cool Pacific night.

Foot-retros eased the pod into a controlled descent; it plunged several hundred feet into the ocean, the thrusters carrying it scarcely half a mile from the fortress to a coral outcropping.

Rico raised the mecha to its feet and initiated a series of booster commands. Thruster flame shot forth from the cockpit sphere as it disengaged from its bipedally designed undercarriage. The three micronized agents were airborne and on their way home.

Had there been a little less preflight commotion aboard the dimensional fortress, perhaps some tech or sentry would have noticed the hole that the agents burned in the hull; but as it was, ship personnel had just enough time to complete their assigned duties let alone check up on someone else's station. And the bridge was by no means exempt from this frantic pace, especially when radar informed them of interspacial disturbances emanating from a region beyond the dark side of the moon.

Lisa was already on the bridge and the captain was just making his crouched entry when the reports began to pour in.

"... We're not sure, but it appears to be the fallout from a massive number of hyperspace-fold operations," Gloval heard someone from radar report.

"Gravity-wave disturbance from the moon," said Vanessa, slender fingers flying over the keyboard to bring schematics to the threat board.

Gloval was standing over her, anxious. "Are they certain it is a fold?"

"It's more severe than that, sir," she told him. "It appears to be multiple folds!"

"Can you estimate the number?"

"Trying..."

"Wait!" said Sammie, and all eyes turned to her. "Maybe they've come in peace this time." Blank stares of disbelief grounded her hopes. "Right," she said, swinging around to her console, "probably not."

That same male voice from radar announced an unidentified object flying directly over the ship.

Gloval turned to Lisa. "Do we have any fighters on patrol?"

"Negative, sir."

"Radar again, Captain. Our monitors show a large alien vessel moving toward Earth from lunar space. It appears to be on a collision or rendezvous course with the object we've been tracking."

Gloval studied the schematic and ordered Lisa to move all Veritech groups to condition yellow at once.

"Picking up a second wave of gravity disturbance," said Vanessa. She gasped as new readouts filled the screen. "I calculate the number of enemy ships to be in excess of . . . *one million*!"

Gloval narrowed his eyes and looked over at Lisa, as if to say: *Yes, your reports to the Council are now verified.* Gloval wanted to see those generals live to eat their words.

"I don't think it matters how many ships the enemy brings in," said Claudia confidently.

"But a *million* of them . . ." said Sammie.

"We'll never be able to outmaneuver them," added Kim.

But Claudia remained undaunted. "We beat them before, and we'll beat them again."

Gloval's thoughts were still focused on the Council. He was certain they were monitoring this latest move by the Zentraedi, and yet there was no word from them.

"Then we're completely isolated," he told the crew.

"Why?" Sammie wanted to know.

The time had come to let them know the truth. Gloval realized that his life for the next twenty-four hours would be filled with many such moments. And yet he couldn't help but ask himself what would happen if he did nothing to counteract the present threat. Had the Zentraedi been pushed beyond their limit? Were they ready to hold the Earth hostage? What did they want, and what would the fools who governed the Council do if Gloval refused to acquiesce to either group's demands?

But Henry Gloval was simply not built that way.

"I guess you might as well know," he began. "The Council has decided that the best way to protect the planet is to use the dimensional fortress as a decoy. We have been ordered to draw the aliens away." He let that much sink in while he moved to the command chair and sat down; then he added:

"This ship and its passengers are considered expendable."

Although Mayor Tommy Luan had at one time expressed concern that Macross had little in the way of newsworthy stories, there was now enough daily news to run morning and evening editions. There wasn't a man, woman, or child in the city who hadn't heard rumors to the effect that the Ontario Quadrant subcommand had withdrawn its offer. Then there were the further exploits of Minmei—*whew*! had that idea ever exploded far beyond his plans!—and, lately, those of her cousin and costar, Lynn-Kyle—one to keep a close eye on for several reasons. And of course the disagreements, quarrels, and fights two months of imposed confinement and stress had unleashed. And tonight

Captain Gloval himself was planning to address the entire ship, as rare an event as had occurred thus far.

Gloval and Lisa had left the remaining preflight preparations to Claudia and the crew, exiting the bridge only minutes after the Zentraedi had made their reappearance on the dark side of the moon. Gloval could simply have raised the ship and put off the address until they were in deep space, but he wanted it behind him. He had no idea what the enemy's next move was going to be, and he planned to ask the residents of Macross for their cooperation and support no matter what course of action he might be forced to take.

They had arrived at the Macross Broadcasting System studios only moments ago, interrupting a live special starring Minmei and Lynn-Kyle. The two cousins, along with Lisa Hayes, stood off to one side of the center-stage podium just now. There were three cameras trained on Gloval; the lights were too bright and way too hot. He was already perspiring under his blue jacket and white cap. He had opted against using the prompter or cue cards, for effect as well as because of failing eyesight. One of the engineers leading the quietly mouthed countdown threw him a ready sign, and he began:

"This is Captain Gloval speaking, with a very important announcement that will affect the lives of everyone aboard this ship. Since our return to Earth, as some of you may already know, I have made numerous appeals to both the United Earth Defense Council and the governing bodies of several separatist states for permission to allow you to disembark and resettle wherever you might choose. I'm certain that you are all aware by now of my feelings regarding your continued presence aboard the fortress. Be that as it may, time and again my appeals have been turned down, for reasons that must remain undisclosed for the present. However, I always felt that progress was being made on those requests, until in light of recent events I have been forced to entertain second thoughts about the Council's position."

Gloval was silent a moment; his throat felt parched, and he began to wonder whether the in-close cameras were picking up the slight tremor of his hands. But he dared not risk looking at himself in the monitors. Rather, he cleared the quaver in his voice and continued.

"My friends and fellow shipmates, I have some very bad news to report to you. I received word just a while ago that this ship and all its passengers have been ordered to leave the Earth immediately."

Gloval heard the cameramen and grips gasp; he imagined a collective gasp rising up from the entire city, strong enough to register on the air supply systems in engineering.

Now for the most difficult stretch . . .

"If we do not evacuate the Earth, we've been warned that we risk attack by elements of our own Defense Forces. I know that you must find this unthinkable, but it is most unfortunately true. You cannot have failed to notice that for the past few days we have been taking on a wide assortment of supplies and provisions. I know it is of minor consolation, but I anticipate that we have enough in stores to undertake the journey ahead. And just where is that? You must be asking yourselves. Well, I will tell you: That journey will be to *victory!*"

Without an audience, Gloval had no idea how it went over, so he risked a quick look at Lisa, who flashed a smile and thumbs up. But were the civilians buying it? Did they still have confidence in his ability to lead them to victory?

Those lights seemed even hotter now; he felt dizzy from strain but pressed on.

"I desperately need all of your cooperation in this moment of terrible responsibility. We must all work for the day when Earth will accept us back. Until then, we will survive as best we can... I give you my most humble apologies..."

No, this can't be happening! he shouted to himself.

But it was: He was sobbing, still on camera and sobbing.

And suddenly Minmei was beside him, her hand on his shoulder. She picked up the mike from the podium and began to speak, the cameras tracking mercifully away from Gloval to close on her.

"Listen, everyone, the captain really needs our support right now. Look, I don't understand politics—after what Captain Gloval has told us, I'm not sure I want to—but I do know that the only way we'll survive this is to pull together.

"We've been on this ship for a long time, and I don't know about you, but I think of the SDF-1 as my home now. Don't forget, we have almost everything here that we could ever have on Earth—our own city and all the things that go along with it. We've all been through quite a bit, but look at how strong we've become because of it. I have more friends *here* than I *ever* did on Earth. You've been like a big family to me.

"Someday we'll return to our real home—we'll never give up hope. But for now, I'm *proud* to be a citizen of Macross City and this *ship*!

"No matter where we go in space or how long it takes, our hearts will always be tied to the Earth. So to help all of us express our feelings at this moment, I'd like to perform a song for you and dedicate it to the Earth we love so dearly..."

And Minmei actually broke into song; white dress swirling, blue eyes flashing, she broke into song. And more than half of Macross joined her. She had touched something. Her words had given voice to some unarticulated feeling the residents of Macross shared. Throughout the city, people shook hands and began to view themselves as a new nation, a new experiment in human social evolution. It was true that many of them had family out there on Earth, but hadn't most of them come to Macross Island in the first place to escape most of what passed for world events? Did anyone really want to be governed by such a heartless group of puppet masters as the United Earth Defense Council?

So they celebrated a bittersweet victory. They shelved their dreams for the last time, and they took a long look around their city, as if for the first time. And many of them crowded to the ports and lights in the hull as the fortress lifted off, Earth already a memory, the unknown ahead.

CHAPTER
SIX

*They [the Zentraedi troops] reacted like adolescents re-
leased from the behavioral constraints of their guardians.
Suddenly there were worlds of pleasure and pure potential
awaiting them—worlds that they'd been denied access to
but that were now theirs for the asking, if not the taking . . .
One doesn't have to look far into the history of our own race
to find examples of the same impulses at work. The so-called
counterculture of late-1960s America comes immediately to
mind, especially with regard to the central place given music
and pleasure, and arising as it did from a decidedly antiwar
movement.*

Zeitgeist, *Alien Psychology*

*"Talk about your 'charms to soothe the savage beast'
[sic] . . . She had enough talent—enough magic—to bowl
over an entire empire! So why not call it as it was?—a Minmei cult!"*

Remarks attributed to Vance Hasslewood,
Lynn-Minmei's agent

THE MILLION VESSELS OF THE IMPERIAL FLEET
formed up on Commander Breetai's flagship, positioning
themselves by rank in the staging area—a multirowed
column of Zentraedi firepower that stretched for thousands of miles into Luna's dark-side space.

In what was left of the command post bowl, Breetai

stood tall and proud, his dwarfish adviser by his side, equally confident for the first time in months. The three returned agents were being regenerated in the sizing chamber, and here was Commander Azonia's troubled face in the projecbeam field. Breetai had already informed her of his reinstatement. Exedore moved to the communicator to check on regeneration status while Azonia offered her reply.

"So I hear," she began. "You've assembled quite a fleet to deal with one small Robotech ship."

Breetai laughed at her sarcasm, gleaming faceplate riding the wrinkles of his grin. "You noticed...that 'small Robotech ship,' as you call it, has caused quite a bit of trouble. Even you, *Commander*, were beaten and humiliated."

"My defeat was humiliating only in that Khyron was responsible for it."

"A good commander keeps his troops in line," Breetai started to say. But Exedore interrupted him deferentially.

"Uh, sir, the sizing chamber...Our agents are ready to deliver their report."

Breetai regarded him briefly, then turned back to Azonia's projecbeam image. "I'll give you your assignment later," he said dismissively.

"But wait, I haven't given you *my* report yet! Miriya Parino has—"

"That will be all," he told her, arms folded across his chest. "More pressing matters require my attention."

"Breetai—" she yelled as the image faded.

"Ah, well done, my lord!" Exedore congratulated

him. He then motioned to the corridor. "I believe they're waiting for us."

"This report may turn the tide in our favor," said Breetai as they left the command post.

Breetai had no reason to doubt that this would be the case. He had no inkling then of the bizarre reversals that were to come not only from his own agents but from another whose micronized presence onboard the SDF-1 was to come as a complete surprise.

Rico, Konda, and Bron, clothed once again in the red uniforms of their rank, were brought to Breetai's personal conference chamber, a sparsely furnished circular room dominated by an enormous exterior bay, currently filled with a view of the Earth and its cratered moon. Central to it was a round table surrounded with comfortable high-backed lounging chairs. The piled artifacts the agents had brought back with them made for a most curious centerpiece.

Breetai reached out and pulled an item loose from the jumble. He regarded it quizzically, its three-legged form misleadingly heavy in his open hand.

"The Micronians call that a 'piano,' m'lord," Rico explained.

"'Piano,'" Breetai repeated. "What function does it serve?"

Rico instructed him to press down on the keyboard of small white teeth. Breetai did so, displeased and strangely disturbed with the noise it emitted. He placed the thing out of reach on the table. Exedore studied it while Breetai hastily examined several other objects.

"Is it alive? Some sort of Protoculture-animated Robotech device?" Exedore wondered aloud.

"No," Rico continued. "It makes music. Music is when different sounds are put together for entertainment. It's really quite interesting when you get used to it. We came to enjoy it very—"

"Explain 'entertainment,'" Breetai demanded.

Rico thought for a moment. "Uhh...diversion, m'lord. This, for example." He selected a small, monitorlike device from the pile and held it up for Breetai's scrutiny. "These seem to provide electronic images in much the same fashion as our own vid-scanners. But several of these can be found in each Micronian quarters for the purpose of observing and listening to 'entertainment.'"

Exedore made a thoughtful sound. "Undoubtedly the means by which they familiarize themselves with battle plans and such. Continue," he told Rico.

But all three agents started to talk at once, excitedly, eager to report their findings. A little *too* eager; Exedore began to worry.

"One at a time!" Breetai said, silencing them. "Don't force me to repeat the threats of our last debriefing."

Rico stood up. "What we brought back represents only a small part of the Micronian society and its customs," he calmly began. "You see, they live a much different life than we do—"

"They're proficient at making repairs within their ship," Konda interrupted, on his feet now and gesturing nonstop. "Indeed, they rebuilt an entire population center on board using only salvaged materials. They adapt quickly to unfamiliar environments—"

"And," Bron blurted out, unable to contain his enthusiasm, "there are many Micronians besides soldiers on board the ship. In fact, they join together many times during the day and move about freely—"

"Males and females are together!" Rico shouted.

Breetai and Exedore, who had been trying to follow these rapid deliveries like spectators at a high-speed tennis match, suddenly turned to each other in near panic.

"Males and females together," Rico was repeating to utterances of affirmation from the others.

"As a matter of fact, it doesn't seem to be as bad as we thought," Konda started.

"We forced ourselves to adapt to the presence of females all around us and were unable to discover any negative side effects," Bron finished.

Already Breetai had heard more than enough, but it went on like this for several more hours before he silenced them again, as confused as he was nauseated by their reports. If the results of the penetration operation had demonstrated anything, it was that further contact with the Micronians could not be permitted. It was obvious that his three agents had been brainwashed by some Micronian secret weapon, and to make matters worse, Exedore was now suggesting that *he* be allowed to investigate Micronian society firsthand!

* * *

Dismissed, the three agents later regrouped in secret at Konda's insistence.

"I kept some Micronian artifacts in my pocket," Konda was confessing to his comrades now. "Did you show them everything you had?"

"No, I held out," Bron admitted. Ditto for Rico.

"Let's see what we've got," Konda said, pulling things from the deep pockets of his red jacket.

Six hands began piling souvenirs on the table, a veritable dollhouse garage-sale assortment of miniatures: a double-burner stove, a small refrigerator, a circular end table, several video monitors, a chest of drawers, a space heater, a commode, a/v discs, CD players, a teddy bear, a set of golf clubs, a guitar.

Konda said, "I'd rather have these than the cruiser commands we were promised."

"I brought along two of Minmei's voice reproductions," said Rico, Minmei's first album edged between his thumb and forefinger.

Bron leaned in to take a look. "How about trading me one of those for something, eh?"

"What piece do you plan to trade?" said Rico, a profiteer's glint in his one good eye.

"I've got a Minmei doll . . ."

"Deal!" Rico answered.

Bron squinted at the album photo of a veiled Minmei.

"You know, the other guys would sure be impressed if they could see this stuff."

Konda was nodding his head. "Yeah, we could get away with showing just a select few, don't you think?"

Within an hour there were eleven soldiers gathered around the table in what had become the agent's clubhouse. Word had spread quickly through the flagship. There wasn't a soldier aboard who hadn't expressed some interest in hearing about the peculiarities of Micronian life, and now that there were, well, *artifacts*— actual objects to handle, look at, and listen to—Rico, Bron, and Konda couldn't have kept them away if they tried. Of the eleven uniformed troops, three were already in dereliction of duty.

The agents passed the artifacts around, pleased to be at center stage to be sure but sincere in their desire to share their experience and adventures aboard the Robotech ship with their comrades. Candies were sampled, objects examined, nuances of Micronian culture explained. But it was soon obvious which artifact among the lot was the hottest property.

"'To be in love,'" sang the doll as it took tiny steps along the tabletop, electronically synthesized voice full of pleasant vibrato, arms in motion, black hair buns like mouse ears.

The soldiers were disturbed, then astounded, but ultimately captivated.

"It looks like a Micronian, but what are those noises?"

One of them, a massive, mop-topped, sanguine-faced brute betraying an uncharacteristic concern, squatted down, crossed eyes level with the tabletop, when the doll tipped over and ceased its song.

"Uh, did I hurt it?"

Konda set the doll back on its feet. "No, dummy. You can't hurt it. It's called a Minmei doll, and that 'noise' is called singing."

"You call that a 'Minmei'?" someone said. "It's incredible—I've never heard anything like it."

"Amazing," said another.

"We should let some of the others hear this."

"Quiet! I can't hear the Minmei when you're talking."

For the remainder of the Zentraedi day, the doll repeated its two-song repertoire over and over again. More and more soldiers stopped by the clubhouse; rap codes and secret handshakes were exchanged, and Minmei's name was being whispered like some password throughout the ships of the Imperial Fleet.

While the "Minmei" continued to gather a secret following among the troops of Breetai's armada, the inspiration for that doll was attending a party at the plush Hotel Centinel, Macross City's best, only a stone's throw from the new skyway overpass. The dimensional fortress had left the Earth, and while most of the city's residents were making the painfully difficult readjustment to life in space, Macross's who's-who were drowning their sorrows in tabletop fountains of recently acquired sparkling spring water and vintage champagne. But this was no sour-grapes affair; it was an all-out bash held in celebration of the premiere of SDF Pictures' first release, *Little White Dragon*, starring Lynn-Minmei and Lynn-Kyle.

The film's financial backers were there, some of the crew, engineers from EVE, the mayor and his crowd, selected extras, and assorted hangers-on. Kyle, too, a little surly tonight but looking dashing in a lavender suit, crimson shirt, and bow tie. But the female lead was conspicuously absent from the indoor merriment, the tables laden with gourmet foodstuffs, the wine and spirits. She had absented herself to the balcony for a breather; show biz was getting to her.

There was a down side to it, she decided. The real thrill was in the performing, the real reward in the applause. But these parties weren't fun at all; they were business, a place for the sycophants and profiteers to gather. This was where they performed, and money was their applause.

Minmei wasn't feeling jaded; it was too soon for that. But she couldn't help but question some of the new directions she was taking, the new directions Macross seemed to be taking. She thought back to the early days, the communal spirit that had rebuilt the city, the family ties that had developed, the sense of equality that had reigned. But things were changing all of a sudden, not only physically—what with skyway ramps, exclusive hotels, and gourmet foods—but *spiritually*. It seemed as though more than a few people had merely given lip service to the idea of SDF-1 "citizenry"; now that existence aboard the fortress was an open-ended reality, those same hypocrites were seeking to claim for themselves the best this place had to offer. A new class system was beginning to form itself, and the last place Minmei wanted to find herself was among a reborn aristocracy. It was so important to stay in touch with one's past, to remember the people who helped you find your place—

"Hey, doll, what's going on?"

Minmei turned from the view to face the sender of that slurred intrusion. It was Vance Hasslewood, her business manager, at least two drinks past his limit.

"You're the star of this party," he said, toasting her with the drink he carried. "You should be inside having fun. What's the problem?"

"Looks to me like you've been celebrating enough for both of us." She didn't bother to conceal her disapproval, but Vance was too caught up in party momentum to catch it. He loosened his tie coyly, eyes closed behind the aviator specs.

"Well, I'll admit that I'm enjoying myself a bit . . . but I've got one heck of a reason. After the movie premieres you'll be a star. We're talking major talent, big, *big* bucks. You'll need two more hands just to haul the money home."

He couldn't have been happier.

"I'm already a star, Vance," Minmei reminded him. "What else can you offer me?"

Vance laughed and put his arm around her. "Hey, it's payday, kid. You want something, I'll get it for you."

"I need a front-row seat for the premiere; it's for someone I want to invite."

Vance made a troubled gesture. "Front-row seat? Now? Those seats were filled weeks ago . . . I don't know Minmei."

She looked directly at him. "Vance. Just do it, okay?"

"All right," he said at last. "I'll see what I can do."

Minmei thanked him, and he wandered off, glass in hand. Smiling suddenly, she leaned her elbows on the balcony rail.

"I wish I could be there to see the expression on Rick's face when I tell him."

Jan Morris was no stranger to people who talked to themselves—she'd talked to herself for years now—but given her present condition it was unlikely that she even heard Minmei's solitary remark. Cocktail glass precariously pinched between her fingers, the former star (and someday mystic) was winding her way toward the railing. Two years in space, self-pity, and drink had taken their toll; she was aged beyond her years, a bleached-blond caricature in long white gloves and strapless gown.

"Minmei, I've been looking all over for you. How are you, dahling? Wonderful party! Having a good—oops!"

Minmei deftly avoided the launched cordial; thick liqueur red as Jan's gown splashed against the retaining wall beside her.

"Excuse me. How *clumsy*, I could just die!" Jan was all false apologies. "Lucky I didn't get any on your dress, dahling. And it's such a *quaint* little dress, isn't it? So full of *charm*; it's really lovely, dear. Did you make it yourself?"

I'll have you know that this lime-green silk cape alone costs more than—Minmei wanted to say. Fortunately, though, she didn't have to say anything, because Jan was already slaloming her way back inside. An older man had appeared and expressed an interest in meeting "the young star of the film," and Jan was now tugging him away from the balcony doors.

"She's not so terribly interesting," Minmei heard her tell him. "Just a child, really. Now, why don't we go sit down somewhere and I'll read your palm."

Minmei was thinking about hiring a bodyguard when Kyle called to her.

"Your manager told me to tell you it's seat A-5. They'll hold the ticket at the box office."

Minmei clasped her hands together under her chin. "Great, Kyle! Thanks."

"Thank Vance," he told her, and led her inside. He had that protective look on his face she'd come to recognize. He placed his hands on her shoulders.

"You've got a big day tomorrow. Why don't you call it a night and I'll walk you back to your room."

"Deal," she answered. "I need to make a call, anyway."

Big day or no big day, there was to be no sleep for her that night. She left a message for Rick at the officers' barracks, but he never called back. The large suite SDF

Pictures had supplied only served to return her to that evening's earlier train of thought. At Vance's insistence she joined him in the rooftop lounge for a nightcap, but even that didn't help. She yearned for her blue and yellow room above the White Dragon, her few possessions, her treasured memories.

CHAPTER
SEVEN

Eventually, Little White Dragon *would find a larger audience, a less involved one to be sure, and critical reaction was mixed, to say the least. More than one reviewer dismissed it as "home movies for the space set"; another called it "low-art therapy . . . propagandist fantasy . . . a misdirected death-wish fable." But several praised it unconditionally as "a prescient warning from the collective unconscious."*

History of the First Robotech War, vol. LXXXII

MIRIYA PARINO, LATE OF THE QUADRONO BATtalion and now an unauthorized micronized operative inside the dimensional fortress, marched briskly down Macross Boulevard. The somewhat Teutonic outfit she had pilfered to replace the sackcloth garment she'd arrived in was well suited to her traffic-stopping martial stride, although she didn't understand what all the stares were about. Perhaps, she wondered, the uniform was inappropriate. If she could have seen herself as passersby saw her—radiant green hair, tight-fitting lavender vest, knickers, white stockings, and high-heeled "Mary Janes" —she would have understood at once.

It had not been an easy week. She had been forced to steal food and moments of rest when opportunities presented themselves. Once or twice she was tempted to accept assistance offered at least a dozen times daily by Micronian males—but thought better of it. Early on she had spotted Breetai's three agents among a crowd gathered in front of a vid-scanner listening to some longhaired male talk of *peace* and *ending the war*! But she saw no reason to make contact with the three and hadn't seen them since.

Peace . . . Micronian ways were baffling, unthinkable. But she was enjoying the challenge. Unfortunately, though, she had yet to find the pilot who had bested her in battle, despite the many soliders she passed in the streets.

Ahead of her now was yet another gathering of Micronians, the largest she'd encountered thus far, and certainly the loudest. Cheering groups of males and females were standing twenty deep in front of a strange-looking building, a backlit message display of some sort jutting out above the entry.

"Little . . . White . . . Dragon," Miriya read aloud, trying out the feel of the words. She knew that the first meant "small" and that the second referred to the absence of color, but she was unfamiliar with the final word.

There was a line of long vehicles with tinted observation ports discharging strangely uniformed males and females in front of the building. The people in the crowd were craning their necks and rising on their toes to catch a brief glimpse of these heroes as they ascended the entry steps, waving and smiling. Adulation was heaped on two in particular: a small dark-haired female someone in the crowd called "Min-mei" and an equally dark-haired male—*the same who had been spouting peace from the vid-scanner!* They were ceremoniously ushered into the building without having to show the passes required by the ordinary citizenry of the population center.

Miriya had little doubt that her quarry was inside, about to be honored for defeating her in battle. It might have even been that long-haired male. Why else would so many attend? She had no pass, but she did have a trick up the sleeve of that white blouse with the ruffled collar. She had noticed that certain facial contortions from a Micronian female could open many a locked door. So giving her thong-laced vest a downward tug, she approached the guard at the gate who was accepting the passes and flashed him her most brilliant smile . . .

Spotlighted center stage inside the Fortress Theater, where an SRO crowd filled the lobby and upper gallery tiers, stood the president of SDF Pictures, Alberto Salazar (chairman of the board of Macross Insurance Company in his spare time), tall and well built, with a thick walrus mustache and blue-tinted triangular shades.

". . . Once again I want to thank you all for your support in the making of this film—the first but certainly not the last filmed entirely onboard the ship. And now, without further ado, I'd like to introduce the stars of the film, Minmei and Lynn-Kyle!"

Salazar made an expansive gesture to the wings, where a second spotlight found the leading couple. They walked arm in arm, acknowledging the applause with a wave or two. Salazar led Minmei to the microphone stand.

"Tell us what it was like to star in your first movie."

"It was thrilling, Mr. Salazar. I just hope the audience enjoys my performance."

The crowd went wild, and Salazar grinned.

"I'd say you already have your answer. Sounds to me like the people of Macross love *everything* you do. And how about you, Kyle? Have you got something to say to all your fans?"

"I just want to thank everyone involved in the production," he began rather shyly. "Especially Minmei, for all the support she's given me. I'm a newcomer to this ship, but I'm pleased to discover how easy it is to make friends here. I'm hoping we can continue to turn out movies to entertain you during our time together. This was a great experience, and I thank you for it."

While Kyle was speaking, Minmei stole a glance at the front row, searching for Rick. She found the mayor, Aunt Lena, and Uncle Max, but A-5 was vacant. *He didn't even call for his ticket*, she said to herself.

But Rick was there all right, pressed shoulder to shoulder with the rest of the standing-room-only crowd in the rear of the theater. He had received the message that Minmei had called but not the part about the ticket reserved for him. There had been no response when he phoned her at the Centinel; she was in fact with Vance Hasslewood at the time, sipping at a kahlua and cream on the hotel roof, thinking about Rick. He was in good spirits nevertheless, happy to be there even when he heard someone nearby say, "I hear that Lynn and Minmei are dating. It wouldn't surprise me if they get married!"

Minmei was singing now, the crowd swaying to her song, and Rick began to move with them, caught up in the moment. *What is this power she has?* he asked himself.

Standing stiffly and in obvious discomfort a few feet away, Miriya Parino asked herself the same thing.

In a review written by two science fiction writers who had been covering the SDF-1 launch for *Rolling Stone* on the day of the spacefold, *Little White Dragon* was billed as "a *kung-fu* fable"; it was to previous martial arts flicks what *Apocalypse Now* was to war pictures. No one would deny that it was an ambitious undertaking from the start, especially for a fledgling company in a three-cinema, fifty-thousand-plus market with little hope for a general release. But it more than fulfilled the expectations of its creators, in much the same way that the Miss Macross pageant had. Financial rewards aside, the film was conceived of as an effort to keep morale high on-board the ship; shot entirely inside the SDF-1 (thanks to the EVE engineers), it created jobs and indirectly helped to perfect some of the "normalizing" techniques used in Macross City.

Set in some undisclosed era of Asian prehistory, the film opens on the barren, evil-looking island of Natoma, where a wizard named Kirc is briefly introduced. The young magician is in possession of a strangely configured seagoing vessel, the bow of which has been fashioned to resemble a dragon's head and neck, the stern a barbed tail. Folded wings form the ship's bulwark and gunwales. It is soon apparent that Kirc is not the rightful owner, and while an army of blood-crazed giants—massive sanguine-fleshed hairless mutants dressed in harem pants, cummerbunds, and vests—move in to repossess the ship, he utters a spell which results in its dematerialization.

Cut to a second island in more familiar waters, tropical and peaceful. Some of the inhabitants become familiar, including the island's resident Zen master and a beautiful girl named Zu-li (played by Minmei, her long hair lightened and braided). Zu-li is a visitor to the island, but after scarcely a month there she is known by one and all. Her quiet songs fill the night air, lulling the inhabitants to sleep and bringing a sense of peace and harmony to everything they touch. Her eventual leave-taking, however, is delayed when a mysterious mist blows in and envelopes the island. Out of this enters the dragon ship.

Most of the islanders are frightened by its appearance, but a band of adventurous men and women led by the Zen master board the ship and bring it in. Zu-li and a

handsome *kung-fu* student named Taiki—Lynn-Kyle—
(a peaceful young man forced by circumstance to fight to
save the people he loves) are among the master's following. On closer inspection the vessel is even more marvel-
ous than its stylized exterior suggests, almost uncannily
lifelike and filled with curious devices the islanders
strive to comprehend.

Time goes by, and on the trail of the ship come the
evil giants seen earlier. Seemingly recognizing the enemy
at hand, the ship defends itself with an outpouring of
fiery dragon's breath that destroys most of the attackers.
Terrified by these developments, the chief orders the
Zen master and his followers from the island. They set
sail aboard the ship and are chased around the world by
the giants in a series of perilous and exciting episodes,
culminating in their attempt to return to their homeland.
Zu-li, meanwhile, has discovered the true power of her
voice: She learns to produce a tone that weakens the
giants while at the same time strengthening Taiki's martial arts skills. He vanquishes enemies the dragon ship
encounters during its long journey home—blue-
uniformed, scimitar-wielding assailants and armored
warriors with bows and arrows—and lays waste to the
giants with *kung-fu* energy bolts and soaring leaps.

In the thrilling climax Zu-li is captured by the enemy
and rescued by Taiki, and the island, which has refused to
allow the journeyers home, is devastated by the giants.

Well before the credits ran, Lisa Hayes left her seat
and exited the theater. That last Technicolor kiss had
been too much for her to take. When she looked at

Lynn-Kyle, she saw Karl Riber; it was Karl's voice she heard when Kyle spoke, Karl's sentiments about war and death . . . Since that first day in the White Dragon she had been drawn to him, moth to flame. He was antiestablishment, antimilitary, antieverything her life had become, and yet she couldn't put him from her mind. She could close her eyes and remember every detail of his face, every word she had heard him tell the reporters about his hopes for peace when all they were interested in was Minmei's health; she could vividly recall standing next to him at the MBS studio the night Captain Gloval addressed the ship; and now there he was, ten times larger than life on the silver screen. *Another giant in her life.* And seemingly in love with Minmei. Minmei again. What magic did she possess? First Rick, now Kyle. It sometimes felt as if the entire ship was haunted by her presence, much as it was haunted by her songs.

Lisa could hear applause coming from inside the theater. Soon the lobby was going to be jammed, and she didn't want to hear everyone talking about how *wonderful* she was, how *beautiful*. She stopped for a moment to glance at the film's colorful glass-encased poster and was about to move off, when all at once someone grabbed her behind! Not a grab, actually, more like a shove! She'd had enough of that waiting on line to get in and was certainly in no mood for it now. Enraged, she spun around, white trenchcoat flying, high red boots and fists ready, *just like in the movies . . .*

And found Rick Hunter groveling on the lobby floor in front of her, apologizing for his clumsiness.

"Commander!" he said, full of surprise. "I *am* sorry. I must have tripped or something..."

Lisa folded her arms across her chest. "And I just *happened* to be within reach, is that it?"

Rick's eyes widened. "Well, what do you think? I can't imagine another reason why anyone would want to, er, grab you."

"That's tellin' her, pal," said someone in the crowd that was gathering around them.

"I don't know, Hunter, first I find you prowling around in a lingerie shop and now you're molesting women on the street..."

"Let him have it, sister," someone else added.

"Shove her again, pal!"

Lisa turned an angry face to their audience and grabbed Rick by the arm. "Come on, Lieutenant, we'd better continue this discussion elsewhere."

That brought out even more comments and a few cat-calls, but Lisa ignored them. She practically dragged Rick down the wide staircase, complaining all the while. "Of all the nerve, intruding on a private conversation like that, how embarrassing, those imbeciles." Appropriately enough, Lisa didn't come to a halt until she had both of them positioned inside one of the black and yellow diagonally striped danger zones. Then she turned on him again. "Now, what in the world were you up to back there?"

"I was just coming out of the movie," Rick said innocently.

"Why didn't you stay to see the ending?"

The blare of warning sirens silenced Rick's reply; he and Lisa looked around. People were already running for shelter, and Sammie's voice was on the PA:

"Attention: Prepare for modular transformation. Please move to the nearest shelter immediately. Avoid the marked danger zones and move to the nearest shelter immediately!"

"A modular transformation?!" Rick said in disbelief.

"Something's wrong. We're supposed to be having a drill. That's why Sammie's on the com."

"A sneak attack?"

Lisa shook her head. "Impossible. Even so, we'd have more advance warning than this."

"We better get to a shelter, anyway." Rick took her arm, but she shook him off.

"Shelter? What's the matter with you? We've got to get back to the base as soon as—"

The street had begun to vibrate and shake. Lisa and Rick exchanged worried glances and hesitantly looked down. Their colorfully striped section of sidewalk was elevating rapidly. They held on to each other as they were carried high above the city streets. Down below people raced for cover. Cars pulled over, drivers and passengers leapt out. The scene in front of the Fortress Theater bordered on pandemonium. Sirens continued to blare and shriek.

The telescoping shaft came to an abrupt stop; then it

lurched into upward motion again, but not before Rick and Lisa had managed to leap off. They were far above the third tier of Macross now, beyond EVE's blue sky illusion in the uppermost regions of the dimensional fortress—an area of massive cooling ducts, recyling conduits, transformational servogenerators, and miles of thick cabling. But Rick thought he knew a way out. He led a skeptical Lisa through a maze of human-size corridors; "portholes" every few feet afforded glimpses of junction boxes and circuit boards inside the walls.

"I think we're near the end," Rick said confidently. "All we do is bear right here."

"You don't say."

"Just follow me. I'll get you out of here. Nothing to it."

A minute later, they were in a cul-de-sac and Rick was scratching his head.

"Nothing to it," Lisa mocked him.

"Must've taken a wrong turn back there."

From somewhere close by came the *click! click!* and hum of activating machinery. There was something about that wall in front of them . . . that seemed to be moving *forward*! They turned and started to run, only to find their exit blocked by a descending hatch. They stood rooted to the floor while one section of wall continued to advance; then, blessedly, it shuddered to a stop.

Lisa breathed a sigh of relief and regarded the thirty-foot-high metal walls of their prison. She dropped her shoulder bag and turned to Rick, exasperated.

"Hunter, aren't you the one who was lost somewhere in this ship for two weeks?"

"Look, how was I supposed to know? We had no choice! Anyway, none of this would have happened if you had gone with me to a shelter like I told you in the first place!"

"That's no way to be talking to a superior officer!"

"What, now you're going to pull *rank* on me?"

Rick made a dismissive gesture and slumped down sullenly against the bulkhead, knees up, hands behind his head. Lisa followed suit in the opposite corner of the box, too frustrated to hold on to her anger. Distant rumblings filtered in.

"Maybe we were attacked," Lisa posited. "Of course, it could be target practice, Phalanx fire or the Spartans ...I wonder how Sammie is doing? She's new at this. But someone has to act as my backup. Claudia has her hands full, and of course Vanessa and Kim..." She looked over at Rick. "You're not listening to a word I'm saying, are you?" No response; Lisa smirked. "Are you planning to sulk for the rest of our time together? You know, you're acting pretty childish, Rick. Come on, damn you, I'm going to go mad in here if you don't talk to me!"

"Well now, there's a surprise," Rick said suddenly. "Lisa Hayes actually needs somebody."

"Just what's that supposed to mean?"

"I figured you were too tough to need anybody."

She glared at him, then softened. "All right, Rick, I'm sorry I exploded back there."

Rick smiled. "Me, too." After a minute he added, "Reminds me of when we were stuck in that holding cell on Breetai's ship."

"Don't remind me. This place looks too much like it."

Rick looked around. "True enough. But even if this ship *was* designed by aliens, it's our ship now—our *home*. We'll just have to wait until she reconfigures."

"If it is a drill, that won't be much longer."

They both grew quiet and introspective; but when another twenty minutes had passed, Rick broke the silence.

"I still can't figure out the Zentraedi's tactics. We haven't scored a decisive victory once. They're always saving us from their own attacks."

"The captain thinks their command is divided. One side is convinced that we're derived from Protoculture; the other disagrees."

"The magic word . . . if we only had some idea what it was."

All at once there was a third voice in the room; Rick and Lisa glanced up and saw a Petite Cola robo-vendor coursing around the upper landing of their enclosure.

"What soft drink would you like?" the machine was saying.

"Hey!" yelled Rick, on his feet in a flash.

Lisa got up and moved to his side. The machine peered over the edge. "We're out of that brand. Please choose again."

Rick shook his fist in the air. "You empty-headed tin can, bring some help! Help!"

"We have ginger ale, Petite Cola, and root beer. Make your selection and deposit appropriate amount." The vendor was circling around making whirring sounds.

"You piece of junk, you no-good—"

"Stop it," Lisa said, tugging at his jacket. "It's not doing any good to yell at it. It's just a machine."

Resignedly, Rick said, "Yeah, I know." He joined Lisa on the floor. "*That* is what Protoculture is all about. Whatever it is that makes those machines behave like idiots."

Lisa laughed. "I don't think so, but we'd have to consult Dr. Lang to be sure."

"No *thanks*."

Again they both retreated to inner thoughts and fantasies, punctuated by muffled explosions from overhead.

"I think Protoculture is more like the *kung-fu* force in the movie," Lisa said at last.

Rick's eyebrows went up. "Oh, so you *were* in the theater."

"Yes, I was there. I know the manager. I had a seat in the back. Why are you so surprised?"

Rick shrugged. "Just hard for me to imagine you at a movie."

"I *do* get out, you know." She felt her anger building again.

"Guess I always pictured you as a shut-in."

"And I picture you as a jerk, Hunter!"

Rick made a show of acting miffed. "But sometimes I can read minds . . ." He put his forefinger to his lower lip in mock concentration. "Let's see, you wanted to see this movie—*even though* it was a chop flick—because you've got a crush on one of the stars."

"Forget it, Hunter," she said, turning away from him.

"Right. You went to the trouble of reserving a ticket and dealing with those crowds just to see a film starring Minmei. No way. It has to be Kyle. Am I right?"

"Back off, Rick. Besides, how do you feel about Minmei now—Minmei and *Kyle*, I mean? You're still in love with her, aren't you? Aren't you?" Rick had lowered his head and grown silent. Lisa apologized. "I was just trying to get you to stop making fun of me. I didn't mean to bring up any bad memories. Believe me, I know what that can be like."

"Then tell me the truth," he said without facing her. "You left the theater for the same reason I did. You couldn't stand to see the person you're in love with kissing someone else?"

Lisa nodded, tight-lipped.

"What a joke," Rick continued. "Both of us running out of the theater at the same time. But how could you fall in love with that guy? He's against everything you stand for."

"He looks exactly exactly like a man I was in love with. *He* had to go away, and then he died before we had a chance . . ." She began to cry in spite of all her efforts to be strong. "Sometimes when I see Kyle, Karl's face comes back to haunt me and I just can't bear it . . ."

Rick passed her his kerchief.

"But where would we be without love?" Rick mused. "Minmei's the only meaning I have in my life."

"You're right, Rick," she sobbed. "But I just don't want to feel this way. I just don't want it."

They held on to each other for several minutes, neither of them speaking.

"I'm glad I'm here with you," Rick told her.

"You're not so bad yourself, Hunter."

"Yeah?"

"Yeah. In fact, I think I could even get to like you—if you could stop being such a chauvinist sometimes."

Rick smiled at her, discovering her eyes as if for the first time. "That's funny, 'cause I was thinking the same about you."

Perhaps they would have kissed each other then—no *alien* pressure this time, no hastily hatched escape plan in mind—but all-clear sirens and Sammie's muffled voice on the city PA broke the spell.

"Attention, please: The drill has ended. The ship will now be returning to its normal mode of operation."

"Time to return to reality," Rick said as bulkheads retracted and hatchways lifted.

Lisa stood up and brushed herself off. "Guess I should get back to the bridge."

Rick got to his feet. "I suppose so. But let's not rush, okay?"

Lisa grinned. "With you leading us, I don't see that we have any choice."

Rick reached out and took her hand. They began to retrace their steps.

There were numerous wrong turns, reversals, and

dead ends, even a few hairy moments and tricky descents; but mostly there was a feeling of togetherness and a fresh spirit of adventure. Ill prepared for the modular transformation and coming as it did with so many people in the streets for *Little White Dragon*'s premiere, Macross City suffered more than its usual share of damage. Rick and Lisa passed overturned vehicles, debris from traffic accidents, and fallen girders and piers in new construction zones. Ambulances and fire crews tore through streets all but deserted now and unnaturally quiet. They would learn later that a mistake had, in fact, been made; what was supposed to have been a simple drill had escalated into a small catastrophe. Sammie still had a lot to learn. Max Sterling, whom the bridge bunnies had spent so much time talking and worrying about, had never even left Macross, let alone the fortress. According to the latest reports, Max was off in hot pursuit of some green-haired beauty in knickers who had caught his eye at the premiere. Minmei and Kyle had left the theater together and hadn't been heard from since.

No sooner did Rick and Lisa arrive on level one near the skyway, when a Petite Cola machine sidled up to them, begging a handout.

"My drinks are undamaged. May I serve you, may I serve you?"

Rick was ready to deliver a few well-deserved *kung-fu* kicks, but Lisa stopped him. She also insisted on paying for the drinks.

"All right," Rick allowed. "But only because I'd like to take you out to dinner next week."

Rick was just removing the cans of soda when he saw Kyle and Minmei walking toward the Hotel Centinel. He pulled himself and Lisa into hiding behind the machine.

"You better stay here," he told her without explanation. Later on he'd feel foolish, but right now he was feeling protective.

"What's going on?" she wanted to know.

Rick was peering toward the hotel. "I didn't want you to get upset."

Lisa gave a look: Arms linked, the leading man and leading lady were entering the lobby.

"Like I said before, welcome back to reality. Guess we'll just have to live with it."

"Look, Rick, let's not worry about them. It's not unusual for cousins to show affection and be close to each other."

Rick snorted.

"Let's get out of here," said Lisa.

"Barracks time, huh?"

She shook her head.

"Let's walk. I don't have to report in until oh-eight-hundred."

"Just you and me?" he gestured.

"Yeah," she said, taking his arm. "Just you and me."

CHAPTER
EIGHT

*Say what you will about the retrospective critiques of
Little White Dragon, it was Breetai's review that mattered
most!*

Rawlins, Zentraedi Triumvirate: Dolza, Breetai,
Khyron

*A world of things we've never seen before
Where silver suns have golden moons,
Each year has thirteen Junes . . .*

Lynn-Minmei, "To Love"(the rallying cry of Rico's
Minmei cult)

"IT APPEARS TO BE SOME SORT OF BATTLE RECORD,"
Exedore was saying.

Breetai agreed. "A primitive fighting style at best. I
don't understand their interest in viewing such a
record."

The Zentraedi commander and his adviser were side
by side in the flagship command post. In the astroga-
tional section of the bridge the rectangular field of the
projecbeam glowed, outlined by the jagged, fanglike remains of the observation bubble. Lynn-Kyle, *Little*

White Dragon's male lead, was up a tree dodging arrows loosed by a small army of bowmen led by a crazed bearded commander with a black eyepatch and a plumed helmet.

"Possibly an instructional requirement for their soldiers," Breetai continued as Kyle's leap carried him out of frame.

Still anchored in space on the far side of the moon, the mother ship of the Imperial Fleet had locked into low-band transmissions emanating from the dimensional fortress. The two Zentraedi had been viewing these for some time, first with puzzled interest and now with growing concern. This long-haired Micronian in the black slippers and belted robe had executed some truly amazing maneuvers, albeit primitive, and now here he was soaring through space unleashing bolts of brilliant orange lightning from his fingertips. The recipient of these, a curiously uniformed hairless mutant wearing some sort of power-collar, was paralyzed and felled a moment later by the Micronian's follow-up leap and kick.

"Did you see what he just did? What was that?!" Breetai was aghast; reflexively he had unfolded his arms and adopted a defensive stance.

Exedore's pinpoint-pupiled eyes were wide.

"Perhaps it is that legendary force the Micronians are said to possess."

"It's a death ray! Our soldiers cannot win against such an incredible force!"

"It seems beyond the power of Protoculture or Robotechnology."

Breetai straightened up decisively. "We must report this information immediately to Commander in Chief Dolza."

Elsewhere in the flagship *Little White Dragon* had a second audience, the dozen or so members of the growing Minmei cult. They were gathered around a monitor screen, jaws slack in amazement. Rico, Bron, and Konda had recognized Minmei in spite of the Zu-li over-the-shoulder braid.

"She doesn't look the way I thought she would," said one of the group.

"Yeah, what happened to your beautiful female?"

"Bubbleheads," Bron said calmly. "This is just a monitor. She's much better-looking in person."

"That's right," Rico added knowingly. "You have to see her in real life. We were hanging out with the girl all the time."

This drew astonished looks from the cultists; they turned now to Konda, who added nonchalantly:

"In fact, the three of us all became her close personal friends for a while."

On the screen, Kyle was going through his F/X routines, dispatching giants left and right and hurling lightning bolts.

Rico recognized him. "These recordings must have been made before the Micronian began to think about putting an end to warfare."

"An end to warfare?" said one of the confused cultists.

"'Peace' is the Micronian word for it," Bron explained.

But what grabbed the attention of this captive audience was the kiss Lynn-Kyle planted on Minmei's lips after effecting her rescue. Cooing sounds surfaced through the speakers.

"How strange," said someone in the audience. "I've never seen anything like that before."

"It's weird . . . Why do they do that?"

"They seem to be enjoying it."

"Yeah," Bron explained. "Something makes them do that all the time. It's required."

"They *make* their people press their lips together?"

"Yeah, it happened every day," Rico answered, ringleader and gifted liar. He had his chair tipped way back, hands behind his head.

One of the heavy-banged clones took his nose from the screen. "That's fantastic! I wouldn't have thought you could stand it. Did they force you to do such a thing with this girl?"

"Yep, they sure did," said Rico.

"Often," from Konda.

Shocked faces, some gray, some yellow, some pure white, swung to catch each spoken word, each nuance.

Then Bron picked up and carried for a while: "My lips got sore from always being pressed."

It has been said that there comes a point in the growth of every powerful cult or movement when something is needed to carry it over the top, to open it up to those who are aware and prepared but who have been afraid to act alone. *Little White Dragon* served this purpose for the Minmei cult. But it had less to do with the "death ray" Breetai saw than with the need to protect the film's leading lady. Singing had reawakened long-lost emotions and impulses; music had reopened a long-locked pathway to the heart.

There was scarcely a soldier in the Imperial Fleet who hadn't heard of the singing doll by now. The film had instilled the rumors with a new momentum; sensational tales of the wonders onboard the SDF-1 were talked about in every corridor and discussed at every watch. The password spread. Micronian words were spoken and memorized. Posts were abandoned, duties left undone. Fights broke out over whose turn it was to carry around the life-size color poster of Minmei. Shock troopers and sentries began to rap on the clubhouse door and beg admittance, their armed and armored presence lending a new element to the gathering of green-uniformed cultists —an element that would soon spell peril for the Zentraedi high command...

The little two-song dot-eyed doll continued to work its tabletop magic, melting hearts hardened by conditioning and countless military campaigns and conquests. Rico's roomful of former galactic warriors came to sound more like a maternity ward visited by a host of proud fathers.

"So this is what they call 'singing,' huh?" said one soldier as he watched the doll go through its motions. "I think I like it."

"Singing is a way the Micronians make each other feel good," Konda explained.

"Makes me feel kinda funny..."

"Makes me feel great!"

"Is it true," asked another, "that we could hear the real singer if we became spies and lived among the Micronians?"

"It's the truth," said Bron.

Rico folded his arms across his chest. "You'd like the real thing a lot more than you like this doll."

"Yes, but it's unlikely that we'll ever get the chance to see for ourselves, Rico. You three are surveillance operatives; we are soldiers."

A grin spread across Rico's face, and he leaned forward conspiratorially, arms on the table. "This is something we should discuss..." he told them.

It is also said that "loose lips sink ships."

Khyron's second in command, Grel, reported to his commander that there was trouble afoot. Khyron had been brooding about his defeat and near death at the hands of the Micronians during the shield explosion and as a consequence ingesting powerful amounts of the dried Flower of Life leaves, so Grel braced himself for the worst.

"You say there's chaos aboard Breetai's flagship?" said the Backstabber disinterestedly.

"That's right, m'lord. Exedore's spies—Konda, Rico, and Bron—returned from their infiltration mission aboard the Robotech ship with a singing doll that is wreaking havoc."

"A 'singing doll'? What are you talking about, Grel?"

"A . . . *device*, Lord Khyron. It emits sounds that have affected the thoughts of the crew. Discipline has become a problem."

Khyron wore a look of distaste. "And you have seen this . . . *device*?"

"No, m'lord, but—"

Khyron turned his back to Grel. "I don't think we need to concern ourselves with rumors."

But Grel persisted. "It's a lot worse than that, sir. There is talk among many of our own soldiers about defecting to the Robotech ship to lead the Micronian way of life!"

Khyron spun around, fists clenched. *"Defecting?!"*

"M'lord!" snapped Grel. "That what I heard. And not just a few—"

"Enough!" shouted Khyron. "Is anyone in the higher command aware of this?"

"No, m'lord."

"As I thought." Khyron sneered. "Everyone is losing their minds over what's happening on the battle fortress . . ." He raised his fist. "Well, let them! Let them perish through their own stupidity! Khyron will survive and prevail! Khyron will live to see that ship destroyed! Khyron *alone* will rule the Fourth Quadrant of the universe! And woe to anyone who stands in his way!"

* * *

It was true that neither Breetai nor Dolza had received word of the incipient desertions, but the commander in chief had reasons of his own for wanting the Micronians annihilated. Breetai had dispatched a ship to the command center with trans-vids of the "death-ray" sequences he and Exedore had viewed. There, Dolza had come as close to fear as his Zentraedi conditioning allowed.

A trans-vid of his response was quickly returned to Breetai. The fleet commander and his adviser screened this on a rectangular monitor that had been installed behind the remains of the spherical one Max Sterling's VT had finished off some months ago. The brief message did not take either of them by surprise.

"I am now convinced that the Micronians have discovered the secrets of Protoculture," Dolza stated flatly. "And as a result they are extremely dangerous to us. Any prolonged contact with them can only have a disastrous effect on our troops. I am therefore ordering you, Commander, to begin preparations for a final assault on the Robotech ship. You are to infiltrate the fortress and secure the Protoculture matrix. Failing that, you are to destroy the ship. And understand me, Breetai: This time I expect results. Succeed or find yourself facing the fury of my fleet."

Word of the impending assault threw the Minmei followers into a state of dismay.

"What do we do now?" asked one of the cultists, Minmei poster in hand. "When we attack the fortress, we'll probably kill this girl. We'll *never* get to hear her sing!"

"We want to hear her sing!" yelled another.

There were at least twenty of them in concealment behind a row of Battlepods in one of the flagship docking bays. All eyes were on Rico now.

"It's not just singing. In the fortress population center they have loads of things we don't have. *All* that will be lost if we attack them!" He struck a determined stance. "Why don't we save them, and save ourselves as well?"

"How?" several voices said.

"We can't do anything by just *thinking* about our future. I say we look for a way to remain aboard the enemy ship when the attack begins."

There was a moment of stunned silence. Even in their weakened state, enough residual conditioning remained to leave them fearful in the face of Rico's suggestion, and more than one forehead was beaded in sweat. But Rico had given voice to their wishes, and soon Bron and Konda were slapping him on the back, full of encouragement and congratulations.

"If they catch us, we'll be executed," said one of the few holdouts.

But Rico was on a roll. "That's the chance we'll have to take," he said, scanning each face.

"Then count me in. I want all those things I've never had before."

"Me, too," said another, and another. Shock trooper

and duty officer alike continued to cast yea votes until it was unanimous.

"Okay. We're in it together," Bron said finally. "But before we can enter the enemy ship we've got to become Micronians."

Again there was a moment's hesitation as the irreversibility of their decision set in. Then someone asked, "Do you know how to work the sizing chamber well enough, Bron?"

"No," he confessed. "It takes a specialist to operate it, right, Karita?"

All eyes focused on a meek, docile-looking blond soldier at the outer perimeter of the group. Nervously, Karita clasped his hands together as Bron put the question to him. It was true. He knew the secrets of control levers eight and nine.

"Without *permission*?" he seemed to whimper.

"Of course, you fool. If the plan is discovered, we're all dead!"

"You want to hear *real* singing, don't you?" said Rico, trying a gentler approach.

Karita turned his back to them and stammered, "Sure I do, but, well, uh . . . ."

Bron took the Minmei poster from someone's hand. "If you help us, this picture *and* the singing doll are yours. What do you say to that deal, Karita?"

"Well . . . I don't know . . . ."

"We've got to work like a team," said Konda. "If we stick together now, we'll all be able to enjoy a new life with the Micronians."

Karita turned to face them. "All right. I'll do it. But you'll have to promise to take me with you."

Bron went over to Karita with a big grin and put an arm around him. "You just operate the converter. We'll see to it that you get into the ship."

Meanwhile, aboard the dimensional fortress life was busy imitating art. *Little White Dragon*, finally shown in its entirety, had received ecstatic praise from one and all, and more than ever Lynn-Minmei's voice seemed to weave a magic spell over the ship. During a follow-up concert carried live by MBS, there wasn't a man or woman who didn't feel somehow *transported* by the star's songs and gentle lyrics. On the bridge Captain Gloval grew introspective, remembering better if not quieter days. Vanessa, Sammie, and Kim, ever-present cups of coffee in their hands, slipped into a sort of collective daydream fantasy where those "silver suns" and "golden moons" were almost tangible and love was something no longer sought but found and embraced. Claudia Grant walked through London snow she hadn't thought about in years, arm in arm with Roy Fokker, her lover still in that interior realm unlocked by Minmei's magic. Even Lisa, who only the day before had walked out on the film, succumbed; but it wasn't Karl Riber she thought of but Kyle, who brought into question all that she had lived and worked for, all that she was.

And from the stage wings of the Star Bowl Kyle watched his cousin perform as though for the first time, feeling at once threatened and comforted, concerned about how much attention was lavished on her and how little was focused on ending the war but at the same time recognizing how all-important Minmei had become to morale and the personal strivings of all those onboard the fortress.

Not for a moment, though, did the singer herself question her gifts or her purpose. Tearfully she accepted the applause, the flowers and love, but in a strangely distanced state of being, as though outside herself, her songs on the side of love in the eternal struggle of good against evil.

And was there anyone more aware of Minmei's cause than Rick Hunter, standing now outside the Star Bowl as she finished one of her tunes, his ear pressed up against one of the posters that adorned the amphitheater wall? *She* was his cause from the beginning, and it seemed certain now that she would be his cause at the end.

CHAPTER
NINE

Although films like King Kong, Attack of the Fifty-Foot Woman, *and* Devil Doll *had understandably enough become popular onboard the SDF-1, perhaps we should have been paying more attention to a little-known classic called* One Touch of Venus, *wherein a statue of the goddess comes to life and sings a song that weaves a spell of love over everyone.*

Lisa Hayes, *Recollections*

THE RIGHT ARM OF ZOR'S SHIP DREW BACK AND hurled itself forward as if it were part of a living being, its steel-hulled supercarrier fist punching through the armor plating of the Zentraedi cruiser and crippling it; only then, with the ship so impaled, was the forward ramp of the carrier lowered and the full firepower of the Micronian Destroids unleashed.

"The '*Daedalus* Maneuver,' as it is called," said Exedore. "Apparently named after the oceangoing vessel itself."

Breetai ordered a replay of those trans-vids which had captured the Micronian battle maneuvers for study: the deep-space destruction of Zeril's cruiser and the fiery death of a destroyer under Khyron's command when the SDF-1 had been temporarily redocked on Earth. Exedore was arguing that it might be possible to *force* the Micronians into employing the maneuver once again, but in such a way as to prove advantageous to the Zentraedi. Breetai was trying to keep an open mind, despite the fact that there was precious little in the way of reinforcing evidence to warrant optimism at this point. If two years of fighting (by Micronian reckoning) had established anything, it was that one could only expect the unpredictable from these Micronians. Still, there was too much at stake to completely rule out Exedore's plan. He had been as shocked by Dolza's threats as Exedore had been. That the Micronians presented an unprecedented danger was not to be argued; but to destroy Zor's dimensional fortress in lieu of capturing it was madness. Without the knowledge contained aboard that ship the Zentraedi would never be able to break free from the yoke of the Robotech Masters. Dolza knew that better than anyone.

Breetai stroked his chin as the trans-vids ran to completion. "We would be taking a great risk," he said to his adviser.

"True, m'lord. But even so, we stand to gain everything if we succeed. If we can force them into executing a *Daedalus* attack, we might be able to insert a Regault squadron into the fortress without detection. Then we would be in a position to capture the ship intact."

Breetai uttered a sound of approval. "That has been my design all along. But how can we make certain the Micronians fulfill their part in this?"

"First, we must rely on the fact that they judge our actions to be as predictable as we judge theirs unpredictable. Then we must take care to so maneuver the flagship that they launch their attack at the bow of our ship. We are strongest there, and with our troops suitably forewarned, it would prove a simple matter to get our infiltrators aboard."

"Hmm... you've thought this out carefully, Exedore."

The misshapen Zentraedi bowed slightly. "May I be permitted to speak freely, m'lord?"

Breetai gestured his assent.

"With the one million ships of the Imperial Fleet at our disposal and Zor's Protoculture matrix in our possession, we would be a force to be reckoned with. Both Dolza *and* the Robotech Masters would have to deal with us."

Breetai grinned. "And what of the Invid? Have you given this thought, too?"

Exedore's pinpoint-pupiled eyes widened at the mention of the name, but he regained his confidence soon enough.

"Those enemies of life as we know it will surely search us out," he told Breetai coldly. "But they will be made to suffer the same fate as the Micronians, and anyone else who presumes to tamper with Proto-culture!"

The flagship sizing-chamber had been the scene of frantic activity since Breetai's sounding of general quarters. True to his word, Karita had operated the reduction converters, secretly "micronizing" some twenty Zentraedi soldiers; and Rico, as promised, saw to it that Karita along with three other Minmei cultists found a place in one of the Battlepods. Sometime later the Zentraedi commanders would learn that fewer Battlepods went out than pilots, but it was not something they needed to concern themselves with at the moment; the Zentraedi were not as fussy about this sort of thing as the Micronians were.

Several conversion kits for the pods had been secured, but not enough to go around. Bron and Konda therefore offered last-minute advice and instructions to the micronized pilots who would be manning the standard pods. Then, in sleeveless sackcloths once again, the three infamous operatives regrouped and climbed aboard the mecha that would deliver them back to the SDF-1 and its world of delights.

Hundreds of Battlepods pressed plastron to plastron filled the launch bay of the flagship. Pilots ran their craft through systems checks and prepared themselves for battle. Rico, Konda, and Bron were at their stations inside the pod when a change in the attack plan was announced from the bridge: All Regault squadrons were being ordered to move to the bow of the ship and await further instructions.

"Now what?" asked Konda in a sudden panic.

"Just calm down," Bron told him, already beginning to move their Battlepod forward with the rest. "The plan is still to attack the battle fortress, isn't it? We'll get our chance, so stop worrying about it."

Aboard Khyron's cruiser, meanwhile, the attack mecha of the Botoru Battalion were readying themselves. The Backstabber's Officer's Pod headed up four shipshape columns of the Seventh's finest fighters. Khyron was addressing them over the net:

"The Micronian ship is almost within range. As soon as their fighters are launched, we will take to space and engage them. Do not concern yourselves with losses; think only of *victory*!"

Khyron lowered the visor of his helmet. *The stage is set*, he said to himself. *Nothing can save the Micronians now!*

From inside the flagship command bubble Breetai ordered his attack force into motion—a relatively insignificant number of ships but appropriate for the occasion. He wanted the Micronian commander to feel confident, not unduly threatened.

"Follow my lead toward the enemy fortress," he spoke into the communicator. And he thought to himself: *Let the games begin!*

* * *

Sammie's scream broke them out of the trance Minmei's songs had sired.

Lisa and Claudia furiously began to tap commands into their console keyboards, while Kim let out a call that brought Captain Gloval running. Vanessa sat hunched over the threat board controls like some maniacal organist.

"Thirty ships," Lisa said, as Gloval tried to make sense of the overhead monitor readout. A schematic showing the fortress's position relative to Earth revealed that a triangular formation of enemy paint had emerged from behind Luna and was presently on an intercept heading with the SDF-1.

"Thirty," Gloval said, puzzled. "Why, when they have so many at their command? What can they be planning?"

"Estimates of TOA and DOA coming in, sir," said Vanessa.

Gloval turned to the threat board and back to Lisa.

"Sound general quarters. Scramble the Veritechs." Gloval took to the command chair and exhaled wearily as alert Klaxons blared throughout the fortress.

Thirty ships, he kept repeating to himself. Not an arbitrary number, but somehow calculated. The enemy was actually communicating with him, offering up just this number of ships as a tease. Not enough to overwhelm the fortress, though just enough for a tight fight. So why was he experiencing such an unusual sense of dread? He couldn't put his finger on the cause, but he likened the feeling to those small warnings your mind transmits just as you're stepping into an accident. Something says "oops!" to you even before you've committed yourself to an action, but your body refuses to listen: It moves forward into catastrophe in some irrevocable fashion, obeying laws of causality as yet unknown.

Gloval stared at the monitor screen, watching the radar blips move closer and closer to the fortress. Well, here was all the advance warning anyone needed, and still he could not bring himself to turn tail. *How that would surprise those Zentraedi bastards!* he said to himself. If he just refused to engage them, if he just set the ship on a course of retreat . . . What response *did* they expect from him this time? he wondered. Once again he would be forced to choose between shield and main gun. Or he could simply wait it out until the enemy began to turn on itself, as had so often been the case. But no, that would go against his training.

Gloval made up his mind that he would simply meet the ships head-on, no second thoughts about it. Brute force against brute force, one on one. He'd bring the *Daedalus* into play if he had to. Just punch those ships from space, one after another. Starting with that lead monster up in lights on the radar screen. Yes, the SDF-1 would start with her: an all-out *strike* to the front of the formation!

Rick was still leaning against the curved wall of the Star Bowl when the sirens went off. He joined a group of VT pilots who had raced from the amphitheater and flagged down a taxi. Together they piled inside and ordered the driver to put the pedal to the metal and get them to the *Prometheus*.

The hangar area was a study in controlled chaos. Pilots ran to their ships, pulling on helmets and cinching harness straps. Flight controllers directed prepped Veritechs toward runways and launch bays, while groups of techs unloaded heat-seekers from antigrav pallets and locked them into undercarriage pylons. Supply trucks and personnel carriers screeched across the floor ferrying ammo canisters and cat officers through the madness, often narrowly missing one another. Shouts and elevator and engine noise erased the gentler sounds of radio communiqués, canopy descent, and rapid heartbeat.

Rick threw himself into Skull One, throwing levers and toggles as he fastened straps and adjusted the seat. The alphanumeric displays of the HUDs and HDDs came to life, glowing brightly as systems ran themselves to self-check status. Rick ran through a self-check himself, then worked the foot pedals and interfaced with the HOL microprocessor, ordering the Veritech forward to the elevator. He had his hands on the Hotas—the so-called hands on throttle and stick—when Lisa appeared on the central commo screen.

"Thirty alien craft approaching from section twenty-four, Skull Leader, do you copy?"

"Affirmative, Commander."

"These aren't ostriches, Rick. Radar shows cruisers and battlewagons. No mecha as yet. Your threat evaluation displays should be registering their signatures now, do you copy?"

Rick turned to a side screen: Thirty bandits in a flying wedge formation were revealed.

"I copy, Commander," he told Lisa. "Locked and loaded; I'm outta here."

"Rick, this looks like a big one, so be careful, okay?"

He pulled his visor down. "You don't have to tell me."

Rick goosed the VT forward at the urgings of a flight controller and positioned it on one of the elevators. He completed his checks as the fighter was raised to the flight deck and stabilized for hookup. As the cat officer and his shooter went through their well-oiled routine, he ran through one of his own.

He summoned up an image of Roy Fokker in his mind's eye, then Ben Dixon. He held on to those for a moment and allowed them to fade in the presence of another. Minmei filled up his thoughts as the VT was catapulted off the hurricane bow of the supercarrier and launched into space.

"Six bandits within range," Rick shouted into the tac net. "Switch over to your targeting computers and fire on my command."

Local space was reduced to a grid on his forward screen, with clusters of Veritechs assigned to each section. Skull One led a formation of five VTs into one of these.

Death, parcelled out.

The enemy pods opened up, disgorging pulses of blue fire into the night. An Officer's Pod was out front—its flashing signature plain as day on Rick's threat evaluation screen—"hand-guns" and top-mounted cannon spewing flame. The Veritechs danced between the deadly lines, thrusters carrying them out of harm's way as nose gatlings blazed a reply.

"Send 'em home, boys!" Rick shouted.

He engaged the VT's afterburners, propelling it farther out in front of the pack. Behind him, one of the newcomers sustained a direct hit and disintegrated in a silent sphere of blinding fire. Two other fighters broke across each other's courses and accelerated into flanking maneuvers on either side of the enemy contingent. Pod gun turrets swiveled to find them without effect, bolts of uncreased lightning telescoping into the void. They broke their formation and scattered in pairs, dangling bipedal legs behind themselves now, boosters blazing pink and white, blue fire erupting from their plastron cannons.

Skull One loosed six red-tipped missiles into their midst, orange crescents and small suns filling the skies as they found their mark. Pods exploded, Human and Zentraedi pilots died, and Death clapped joyfully from the sidelines.

It was a free-for-all, rockets and pulsed beams crosshatching space haphazardly. No one was safe, no one immune.

Inside the flagship Breetai watched the battle from his

command chair, Exedore stone-faced beside him. The
fleet commander was pleased.

"So far they are following their usual attack pattern."

Off to the right of the observation bubble, two indicator lights flashed on. Breetai and Exedore turned to
these.

"This is operations," said someone from the launch
bays. "All our Battlepods and mecha have been deployed."

"Good," Breetai responded, directing his words to the
communicator. "Inform all the cruiser commanders that
I want them to continue on course. But make certain
they allow the flagship to maintain the lead."

"At once, my lord," came the reply.

Breetai rose from the chair. "Prepare to fire main batteries."

Pinpoints of blue light flashed into life across the front
of the cruisers; bursts of pulsed energy rained from the
front of each of these, regular as clockwork.

Meanwhile, pods and VTs continued to slug it out.
Rick found himself up against that Officer's Pod again;
the enemy mecha was in ascent, thruster glowing between its legs while it exchanged fire with Skull One and
its wingships. Aft and slightly port, a VT exploded—one
of the less-armored tan and white ships piloted by yet
another newcomer. Engaging the undercarriage and lateral thrusters, Rick piloted the VT up and over the
enemy fusillade; one of his wingmen followed but was
tagged and blown to debris. As enemy fire mysteriously
ceased, he cut away from the silent Officer's Pod and

went after one of the regulars, executing a Fokker Feint, then rolling over and taking it out with gatling blasts while it floated stationery in space. The Officer's Pod tracked Rick as he completed the move, encasing Skull One in streaks of fire from which it emerged miraculously unscathed.

The SDF-1, however, was not faring as well. While the VT teams were successfully shielding it from the stings of enemy mecha, the fortress was sustaining salvo after salvo from the rapidly approaching whalelike ships of the attack group. Bristling guns discharging unbroken lines of lethal energy, the warships closed on the SDF-1 like deep-sea monsters in a feeding frenzy.

The massive ship was shaking violently. On the bridge Captain Gloval gripped the arms of the command chair for all it was worth. The women worked feverishly at their stations, tireless and unfailing in their duties, the occasional scream notwithstanding.

"Damage reports coming in, Captain," said Kim.

"Later!" he answered.

Claudia reported that the Veritech teams were taking heavy losses.

"Keep them deployed as long as we can!" Gloval shouted to her as an explosion rocked the bridge. "Lisa, we're going to have to use the *Daedalus* to take out those cruisers one by one!"

Lisa turned from her console to signal her understanding, then reached up for the remote mike cradled alongside the overhead monitor.

"Stand by to launch *Daedalus* when you receive my command," she said.

Full of sinister intent, streaks of light radiating from what looked like eye pods and the suggestion of a mouth turned up in a crooked smile, the Zentraedi flagship continued to bear down on the fortress. Concealed behind bulkheads and hastily erected reinforcing partitions in her bow waited scores of Battlepods, erect on their hooved feet, turret guns aimed and ready.

Inside one of the pods the three operatives received word of the imminent Micronian counterattack. Rico and Bron were standing on the seat, each positioned at one of the projecting levers that controlled the mecha. Konda was down below near the foot pedals. Bron held a communicator in his hand; through this he was in touch with the rest of Rico's band of micronized would-be deserters.

"Are you ready?" he said into the mike. "Our moment has arrived."

"To our deaths, or our rebirth!" said Rico in a rallying cry.

The three raised their hands in salute to one another.

Rico grew serious. "Once inside the fortress, we'll have to take care."

"The wrong place at the wrong time and we could be killed—by Micronians or Zentraedi," cautioned Konda. "We'll have to stay out of sight until the proper time. Then we'll abandon the pod and lose ourselves among the people of the population center."

"He's right," said Bron getting back on the mike. "I'll pass the word."

The Macross Amphitheater was shaking and quaking —not to thunderous applause or the rhythm of the band but to the frenzied beat of war. Half of the Star Bowl's 30,000 had fled for shelter at the first warning sirens, and many more began to filter out as the sounds of battle invaded the ship, but a surprisingly large number remained—mainly those who were guided by the past, the unfortunate ones who continued to believe that Macross would always be immune to attack.

Minmei was introducing a song when the first major jolt was felt. She cried out as she almost lost her balance, and this started a wave of panic in the audience. Suddenly the diehards and risktakers were having second thoughts. People were screaming and rising halfway out of their seats in dismay, as if to get a general fear-level reading before making up their minds to exit or stick it out.

Kyle could almost smell the panic brewing. He took to the stage in a leap and ran to Minmei's side.

"Minmei, you've got to keep singing," Kyle told her.

Only moments before he had been watching Minmei's performance from the wings, fascinated by how her mere presence could overshadow the war. And now he glimpsed a way that her power might be put to good use in lulling the audience back into a state of calm.

She turned to him, panic in her eyes, smudges of run mascara beneath them. "What?" she said, not comprehending.

"Gimme that," he said, taking the mike from her hands. "Hey, everybody, we're going to continue the concert, so please take your seats. There's no reason for panic. We've all been through this before. So please calm down and return to your seats. Minmei's going to go on with the show."

Another jolt rocked the ship, and the screaming escalated. Minmei had her hands over her ears, but Kyle was shaking her by the shoulders and telling her to sing.

"In your strongest voice!" he told her.

She looked up at him, wide-eyed and childlike, but nodded her head.

"Be courageous and sing," Kyle said calmly. "You can do it."

Reluctantly she took the mike and stepped forward on trembling legs. She walked out of the stage's inlaid five-pointed star and perched herself on the edge. The band, taking this as a cue, gave her an intro. She motioned them to pick up the tempo and began to belt out "Stage-fright." People returned to their seats. Minmei turned and winked at Kyle. He smiled at her and mouthed: "You're great!"

On the bridge, Lisa Hayes gave the word. With a little luck the destruction of the lead ship would result in an explosion that would take out the others as well.

In space the right arm of the SDF-1 drew back and hurled itself forward, as if it were alive . . .

CHAPTER
TEN

> *"What you fail to grasp is that Commander Breetai's de-*
> *cision to allow the SDF-1 to retreat was entirely in keeping*
> *with the Zentraedi tradition of open warfare, that is, move*
> *and countermove. It was most certainly not a tactical*
> *blunder...Moreover, it is for precisely this same reason*
> *that it never even occurred to Commander in Chief Dolza to*
> *hold the planet Earth hostage for the return of Zor's ship.*
> *Through no fault of your own you imagine this to be unthink-*
> *able. Which, then, is the more barbaric of the two races—*
> *yours or mine?"*

> Exedore, as quoted in Lapstein's *Interviews*

THE STEEL-PLATED BOW OF THE SUPERCARRIER *Daedalus* punched through the nose of the Zentraedi flagship.

It was an encounter of mythic proportion, worthy of
inclusion in that short list of eternal struggles—angel
and demon, eagle and snake, snake and dragon: *a giant
techno-knight in gleaming armor, its fist locked in the
jaws of a deep-space armored leviathan...*

The two-foot-thick bow plate of the *Daedalus* swung
up and away from the body of the ship, its massive top-

mounted hinges groaning in protest. Unseen servode-
vices locked while others disengaged, motors whined,
and hydraulic couplers hissed in a symphony of mechan-
ization. A triple-hinged forward rampart unfolded itself
into the hold of the Zentraedi ship while a fan of brilliant
energy was lossed from Destroids in the carrier belly.
Structural piers and pylons were blown away; girders
and tie beams slagged in the infernal heat. Supply crates
and storage tanks exploded, filling the air lock with con-
cussive sound and deadly fumes. A bulkhead just inside
the breach was holed by concentrated firepower.

Golden alloy-armored Destroids now began to de-
scend the ramp, their lasers at rest. They were early
products of Robotechnology, bipedal and nearly as tall as
Battloids but somewhat cumbersome-looking, with large
square feet and skeletal laser-gun arms. Following their
programmed directives, the three-man units moved into
the hold and took up positions for a second and more
lethal assault. But they were not quick enough.

Battlepods suddenly leaped from places of concealment and opened fire. Pulsed beams tore through the
thin skins of the mecha, dropping them in their tracks.
There were attempts to return fire, but the situation was
instantly beyond hopeless. The Destroids were vastly
outnumbered and easily overrun; minutes after the skirmish erupted, their silent forms were heaped at the base
of the ramp.

Then the Battlepods reversed the order, taking to the
ramp and making for the *Daedalus*. By this time, however, word of the defeat had reached the carrier com-

mand center, and the arm of the SDF-1 was already re-
treating, ripping out the steel tendrils the flagship defense systems had attached to it in an attempt to seal the
breach. There was barely time enough to insert a quarter
of the battle-ready pods. As the final few hopped grace-
lessly into the carrier hold, the ramp folded, retracted,
and slammed shut.

The Zentraedi had been given no clear-cut orders,
save to enter the Micronian ship and inflict as much
damage as they could without destroying it. Breetai's
hope was that at least some of the pods would make it to
the bridge of the fortress and effect a capture of the commanders. Short of that, the pods could attempt to inca-
pacitate the ship's reflex drives.

Some of the Zentraedi soldiers, however, had their
own ideas.

Once inside the *Daedalus*, in an orgy of indiscrimi-
nate destruction, they began to fire at everything in
sight. Provisions, mecha, vehicles, and Gladiator teams
were wiped out. Techs left their stations and picked up
weapons to combat the intruders, but not one lived to
give details of the battle. The Zentraedi hurled fire
against the control towers and communications stations,
incinerating systems and personnel with equal abandon.
The hangar areas of the carrier were fully aflame by the
time the pods took to the main corridors of the SDF-1.

They still had no idea where they were going, but it
was easy enough for anyone to tell where they had been.
A path of utter destruction led from the supercarrier, up
through the right arm of the fortress and into its heart—

Macross City itself. The pods moved wantonly through service corridors, extending their reign of death. Coveralled techs were fried by bolts of unleashed fury; shaking hands reached out weakly for comlink phones and panic buttons but seldom found them. Meanwhile the pods continued their sweep. The Zentraedi were finally repaying the Micronians for two years of frustrating defeats. The mecha soldiers were so caught up in vengeance that not one of them noticed the disappearance of several of their number—a group of awkwardly piloted pods that seemed curiously loath to engage in battle.

Captain Gloval's leg shook uncontrollably while he awaited Lisa's reply. "Come on, Lisa, come on," he said, hoping to hurry along the flow of data.

She was bent over her console, fingers flying over the keyboard. "I have no contact at all with the *Daedalus*, sir. It's as if it doesn't exist!"

Something was very wrong. The oblate bow of the Zentraedi warship filled the bay of the bridge, dark green in color, menacing, enormous. It looked to Gloval as if a whale had mistaken the arm of his ship for a giant fishhook. But the calculated collision had not worked out as planned. Whatever the firepower unleashed by the Destroids, it had not been sufficient to affect the cruiser. In fact, the ship was still hurtling forward, now pushing the fortress along in front of it. And the bridge had lost contact not only with the Destroid squad but with the entire supercarrier garrison as well.

"Pull the fortress back!" Gloval shouted suddenly. "All power astern and redeploy the shield energy!"

As Kim and Sammie relayed continued commands to engineering and astrogation, the fortress began to vibrate to a steady bass drone. The engines were powered up and engaged; then the contained explosive fire of the reflex core erupted from the ports of the pectoral thrusters, carrying the ship away from its aggressor, pulling the *Daedalus* arm free of the flagship's hold.

Gloval breathed a sigh of relief.

The fortress responded with an unprecedented sounding of Klaxons and alert sirens.

Claudia was on the comlink; she lowered the handset and turned to face the command chair, a look of unmitigated terror contorting her face.

"Enemy Battlepods have entered the ship through the ramming arm!"

Gloval's eyes opened wide. "The enemy's on board?"

This had happened only once before, when an overeager Zentraedi pilot had given chase to Max Sterling's Veritech and battled it briefly in the streets near Macross General Hospital.

"The *Daedalus* is on fire," Claudia continued. "The pods are attacking Macross!"

"Quickly! Patch us into the civil defense network!"

The captain and his crew turned their attention to the speaker system, hoping against hope.

"Ten enemy pods on Lilac Street," said a horror-stricken voice. "We're trying to hold . . . *Aargh!*"

"This is area B control—we can't seem to hold them back, we need help—"

"...retreating from the Tenth Avenue gate. We're getting our—"

"Switch it off!" Gloval shouted from the chair. He dropped his head and said weakly, "God help us all."

Destroids, Spartans, and Gladiators were waiting for the Battlepods when they reached the outskirts of Macross City. For those battle-weary residents who had yet to reach shelter, the attack would recall a similar one two years earlier. But this time they knew their enemy. This time they knew how much they had to fear.

Bent on nothing less than complete destruction, the pods advanced through the street, blue fire spewing from their upper and lower guns, panicked pedestrians scattering beneath their hooved feet. Explosions launched fragments of glass and steel into the artificial air and tore gaping holes in the streets, exposing raw power lines and rupturing water conduits. Raining showers of electrical sparks, store signs dangled dangerously from fractured rooftops. The facades of buildings fell and burned, sending up clouds of dust and thick smoke.

A pod, its twin guns blazing, stepped out from behind the remains of a clothing store to face off against a Gladiator positioned at the end of the block. Bursts of blinding fire were exchanged again and again until both pod and mecha exploded, while elsewhere rockets fell and flames spread. A massive multibarreled autocannon swept along Macross Boulevard, sending ground-to-air heat-seekers against airborne mecha. EVE's star-studded sky veneer was stripped away, revealing in stark detail the naked terrors of war.

Not all the pods were blasting away, however. Some were actually looting the shops for souvenirs, raking in whatever appeared intact with the mecha's grappling hooks and waldo gloves. Two of the pilots got a fix on an external sound source that was similar to Minmei's "singing"; and the pair moved off together, homing in on the Macross Star Bowl.

Inside, Minmei was still on stage, wedded to her audience in some sort of unrehearsed litany of song.

Without accompaniment, she sang, "To be in love..."

And they chanted: "Stagefright, go'way, this is my big day."

She was grasping the mike tightly in both hands, though she was certain that the power had gone off. But her face betrayed no fear. Kyle was standing stiffly by her side, his fists clenched, urging her to go on. From what she could tell, the city beyond the amphitheater rim was engulfed in apocalyptical flames; thick black smoke was billowing toward the ceiling of the hold, and a light rain seemed to be falling from the overhead water-retrieval system. Electrical power had shorted out in most areas of the stadium. The spots were off. The band had fled. And those in the audience who weren't singing were crying. It felt like the end of the world.

Then, all at once, two Battlepods appeared on the upper tier of the amphitheater, their cannons aimed ultimately at the stage, and she dropped the mike.

Kyle stepped forward and raised it again to her mouth.

"You've got to continue singing, Minmei. Give it all you've got!"

He put his arm around her, and she found the courage to pick up where she'd left off. The audience followed her; she believed they would have followed her anywhere.

"Now, don't be afraid," Kyle was saying into her ear. "They're not going to hurt us."

And it truly seemed that way for an instant—as if the pods were just part of the audience—until a bolt of blue energy flashed overhead and struck the upper reaches of the stage canopy. It had not been launched by either of the pods and was in fact a stray shot from outside the amphitheater. But that made little difference. The crowd panicked. And worse still, the blast had loosened one of the large overhead spotlights. For a second it looked like it wouldn't fall. Then something snapped and gave way, and down it came.

Kyle spied it in the nick of time and moved in to cover Minmei. He succeeded perfectly, taking the full force of the impact on his back, the spotlight driving both of them violently to the floor.

Outside the fortress, things were not much better. The SDF-1 had managed to put some distance between herself and the Zentraedi warships, but furious space dogfights were continuing. Rick was locked into the vacuum equivalent of a scissors finesse with the Officer's Pod that had been hounding him since the word go. Each time he tried to break or jink, the pod stuck to his tail, loosing cannon fire, and now here was Lisa on the right commo screen vying for his attention. Fortunately, Max had been monitoring the aircom net and was coming in to give Rick some relief. Sterling came in low under the Officer's Pod and chased it off with Stilettos; Rick angled himself out of the immediate battle arena and went on the net to the fortress bridge.

"*In* the ship?" Rick repeated in disbelief.

Lisa reaffirmed it. "They're destroying everything, Rick. Return to base immediately!"

Minmei! Rick screamed internally. "Lisa, have they hit the amphitheater? You've got to tell me!"

"I don't have a status report, Rick. Just get back here on the double."

As she signed off, Max appeared on the left screen.

"I'm with you, Commander," said Sterling. "I'll follow you home."

Which was easier said than done.

First the two Veritechs had to navigate a web of pulsed fire laid out by the Officer's Pod and its three cohort ships, then direct themselves through the continuous bombardment the fortress was receiving from the enemy warships. Rick raised the bridge and asked Lisa to see to it that one of the SDF-1's ventral docking ports was opened for their entry; it would have been not only a longer route to Macross via the *Daedalus* or *Prometheus* but a more dangerous one as well. No one in fact had ever *piloted* a VT through the arms of the fortress.

Rick rehearsed his moves as he closed on the air lock; he visualized a map of the city streets and began to plot a course, almost as if allowing the mecha to familiarize itself with the plan.

Skull One and Skull Two zoomed into the fortress, unaware that four Battlepods had followed them in, Khyron's Officer's Pod in the lead.

Miriya was as surprised as anyone to see Zentraedi mecha in the streets of Macross City, and just now she was possibly the only person alive in those streets. Most of the Micronians had taken to the shelters long ago, but many had remained in the amphitheater to witness the workings of some sort of psychological weapons system. For some unknown reason the Battlepods had also chosen to concentrate their might there, and as a result the Micronians had sustained heavy personnel losses. In addition the pods had laid waste to much of the surrounding city. Fires continued to burn, explosions could be heard and felt from all quarters, and a steady rain of embers, soot, and debris fell from the ceiling of the enormous hold.

Miriya had been one of those who remained unsheltered in the amphitheater. She had been trailing the long-haired Micronian warrior ever since the populace had turned out in such force to honor him at the trans-vid screening of his battle records. It seemed likely that the female warrior shown in those trans-vids was the same one who had drawn such a fanatical following to the amphitheater. The vocal noises she emitted had been discomfiting; they had left Miriya feeling debilitated and ill at ease, much as she had felt upon recognizing that the female warrior was in some way the *consort* of the long-haired male!

Until moments ago Miriya had been convinced that the male warrior was the one who had defeated her in battle, but something had happened to alter her thinking. She had seen him crushed by the falling illumination device and, while working her way down the aisles toward the stage, had spied a blue-trimmed Micronian fighter streak overhead. Certain that she recognized the mecha, she had taken to the devastated streets to watch the pilot of that ship in action against her allies.

The fighter was reconfiguring to bipedal mode now as she watched, fascinated, from her place of concealment. The pilot was about to bring the gatling into play. Surrounded by pods, he twisted and trap-shot one from the air, then spun around and took out a second that had landed behind him. Agilely sidestepping the blast of the exploding pod's foot thruster, he utilized the earned momentum to position himself for a bead on a well-situated third. Yet another pod mistakenly thought that height would be advantageous and lifted off, foot thrusters blaring and top guns blazing away. But the Micronian merely sent his mecha into a beautifully executed tuck and roll and came up shooting as the pod came down beside him. Again the foolish Zentraedi pilot tried to leap and fire, but the blue ace had already decreed his fate: Bolts of lightning striking around him, he raised the muzzle of the cannon, fired, and holed the pod with a shot right through the front viewscreen. While the mecha blew to pieces in midair, the Micronian set off in search of greater challenges.

Miriya was depressed by the Zentraedi pilots' poor showing—it was no wonder Breetai's troops were losing!—but elated at having at last discovered the object of her long search. Now she simply had to hunt him down and confront him.

Elsewhere in Macross Rick had also set Skull One down in Guardian mode and reconfigured to Battloid, shooting his way to the Star Bowl area of Macross, where the fighting was thickest, charging down city streets he knew so well and closing on the amphitheater. He had literally just bowled over two stationary Battlepods when Max raised him on the tac net.

"How bad is it where you are?" Sterling wanted to know.

Rick panned his external cameras across the burning cityscape to take stock of the scene: There wasn't a storefront left undamaged—it looked as if some of them had been *looted*! The streets were torn up from explosions and the hooflike feet of who knew how many enemy mecha. EVE's "sky" had taken a beating—most of it had in fact fallen—and few of the deadly fires had been brought under control.

Rick went on the net: "It's worse than I even thought, Max."

"Any civilians about?"

"None that I can see," Rick answered, calling for

zoom on the scanners. "Looks like most of them made it into the shelters."

Static crackled through Skull One's speakers.

"Same out here. What's your next move?"

"I'm going to check the Star Bowl. See that everybody got out of there all right."

"Minmei . . ."

"Right, Max."

"All right, Skull Leader, I'm signing off. Rendezvous with you at the Star Bowl. Over and out."

Rick took a deep breath and relaxed back into alpha. He hit the foot pedals hard and began to think the mecha back into a jog. Enormous explosions erupted behind him as he started out, the gatling in the Battloid's right hand, metalshod left clamped on the cannon for added stability.

Rounding a corner at a good clip, he ran smack into heavy fire. Several pods had taken to the rooftops here and were throwing blue bolts at anything that moved. Up ahead a grounded pod sustained a hit in the back and keeled over as Rick approached. Rooftop rounds were impacting all around him, and he was forced to dive Skull One sideways to the street, left arm straight out for counterbalance as he went into a double roll. The muzzle of the gatling was up before he completed the move, just in time to sear off the right leg of a pod that had leapt from an upper-story support. The enemy mecha rolled over on its back, flame blazing from what was left of its leg, and exploded.

Meanwhile Rick was back on his feet again and already resuming his pace. But not fifty meters down the street a pod stepped from the shadows of a department store doorway and almost succeeded in nailing him. At the last minute, Rick saw it and launched the Battloid like a high jumper over blinding flashes of cannon fire. As he rolled into a front flip, he opened up with the cannon and caught the pod between the legs, transuranic slugs lifting it off the street before it burst to pieces in a ball of orange and purple flame.

Skull One landed hard on its back, smoking gun still clutched tightly in its right hand.

Inside the cockpit Rick shook his head clear and found himself staring straight up at a gaping hole in the hold overhead and two more rooftop pods that were now pouring rounds at him. He thought his mecha into a roll and twist to the right, which ultimately brought it to a kneeling position, the muzzle elevated and armed. Trigger finger on the Hotas, he squeezed, bringing the mecha's left hand up and around to fasten on the forward section of the gatling. The street quaked as explosive-tipped projectiles spiked into the area around him.

Rick sprayed the pods right to left seemingly without effect, the gun sputtering and overheating in the Battloid's grip. Then it gave out completely. But after a moment of dramatic stillness, the pods fell headfirst from their ballet poses on the building ledge. Trailing fire, they crashed on either side of Skull One, fulminating.

Thinking the Battloid erect, Rick shouted, *"Minmei!"* and continued his charge on the amphitheater.

CHAPTER
ELEVEN

I can't imagine what he was thinking when he grabbed me like that, pinning my arms and forcing himself on me. Why do they all have to fall in love with me? Why do they all need to possess and control me? ...All I could think about was what happened on Thursday, when Kyle saved me from falling into one of the modular transformation troughs and I looked up and saw Rick's face in place of his.

From the diary of Lynn-Minmei

A kiss is just a kiss.

Mid-twentieth-century song lyric

KHYRON AND SIX OF HIS FINEST SWAGGERED THEIR pods down Main Street, mopping up what was left of the civil defense patrol Battloids and Gladiators. The Backstabber couldn't have been happier. The fortress's population center was in flames, Zentraedi mecha were overrunning the last few remaining pockets of resistance, and soon the heart of the ship would be secured. It would only be a matter of time before they moved against the ship's command centers.

"Victory will be mine!" he shouted from within his Officer's Pod.

But something was about to occur that would rob Khyron of this false apotheosis, something that would give new meaning to his nickname...

"Destroy everything in sight!" he commanded his troops. "We can do anything we want this time!"

Two Battloids suddenly appeared in the distance; they had taken up positions on either side of the street a few blocks ahead and were now leaning out from behind buildings, directing pulsed cannon fire against Khyron's methodical advance. But the Zentraedi commander never even broke stride; he casually took out both of them with hand-gun hip shots.

He was beginning to increase the pace somewhat when three Battlepods darted out across his path from a perpendicular side street with an obvious purpose in mind. Khyron signaled his own troops to halt and opened his comlink to these preoccupied pods.

"Just a moment," he said, stepping forward, his voice full of suspicion. "Where in the name of Dolza are you three going? Answer me at once!"

The three pods stopped and turned to him. Vocal salutes and sounds of surprise came across the net.

"Respond!" Khyron repeated.

After a moment one of them said, "We are hoping to find Minmei, Commander."

"Minmei?" Khyron said uncertainly. "I've never heard of a Minmei. What are its ballistic capabilities?"

"She's not a missile, sir," said another. "She's a Micronian female!"

All at once the three of them were laughing with delight. Several other pods had skulked out of the side street to watch the exchange.

"The most incredible creature in the universe!"

"We've got to meet her in person. Hear her sing—"

"Silence!" Khyron cut them off.

The pods snapped to, but muffled laughter continued. Khyron narrowed his eyes. So the rumors Grel had reported were true, he said to himself. Defection: It was unheard of.

Khyron's voice dripped menace when he spoke again.

"I presume you plan to tell me what you're laughing about."

"I'm sorry, m'lord," one responded, attempting to stifle his laughter, seemingly unaware that Khyron was bringing one of his hand-guns to bear on him. "It's just that I'm so overcome with joy at the possibility of finding Minmei—"

Khyron fired once, his round entering the pilot chamber through the central viewscreen and exploding.

"He's out of his mind!" Khyron heard over the comlink as the pods ran for cover. "Run, run!"

"Stop!" he commanded them, looking around and realizing that even members of his own crack unit were abandoning him. "All of you, come back!"

Khyron threw his pod into Pursuit mode, hooved feet pounding along the city streets. Not one of them would live to see the end of this day, he promised himself. Already he had one of the deserters centered in his top-cannon reticle.

"Come back here, soldier, and face me like a Zentraedi! You can't run from me forever!"

"I'm sorry, my lord," came the meek reply over the net, "but I—I can't explain what *joy* it is to be among the Micronians."

"What?" Khyron shouted. "I've never heard anything so crazy in my life! You're completely *mad*, do you hear me? You're telling me that you'd prefer to be with *them*?!"

Khyron heard an exclamation of fear but no explanation. He shook his head knowingly and pronounced sentence as the chase continued: "Well now, my little friend, I'm afraid I must deal with you in the same way I dealt with your companion."

The Officer's Pod right hand-gun fired once. The pod took the hit in the rear end, was lifted up as though goosed by fire, and was blown clear from the street.

Khyron fired again and again, pursuing the Battlepods through the ruined streets into the city's night.

Minmei summoned her strength, heaved once, and managed to drag herself out from under Kyle's dead weight. She felt bruised and mangled, and her red gown was in a sorry state. The large canister spotlight that had beamed her cousin was several feet away, tipped over on its side amid plaster chips, shards of plastic, and other bits of fallen debris. The amphitheater appeared to be deserted, but there were flames and thick smoke in the distance and the sounds of sirens and explosions.

Wondering just how long she'd been out, she began to tuck stray hairs back into their bunlike arrangement. Kyle made a groaning sound, and she went over to him, helping him to his feet and walking him to the wings, where they both sat down. He was breathing hard, and his forehead was cut. Minmei took a handkerchief from his pocket and dabbed at the blood. As he came around, she said, "I'll make it better," and started to make funny faces for his benefit. She crossed her eyes, stuck out her tongue, puffed out her cheeks, uttered some strange sounds, and in a minute had him laughing.

"There. All better," she announced in a motherly tone, stroking his face with the kerchief.

Had she been less concerned about what was to prove to be a very minor injury, perhaps she would have noticed the look that began to surface in his dark eyes and would have been able to avoid the awkward scene that followed.

Kyle was so used to taking care of himself that Minmei's attentiveness overwhelmed him. In his still weakened state he found his feelings for her confused but undeniably powerful. She was so much stronger than he had ever thought possible, so talented, such an amazing *presence* in the lopsided world they inhabited together...

So he expressed these thoughts and feelings the only way he knew how: He reached out for her and kissed her full on the mouth.

They were kneeling face to face on the stage; it was dark, and maybe he didn't see her eyes go wide with bewilderment and fear—or maybe he just didn't care. Perhaps he somehow misread her attempts to push him away. But it is more likely that he pinned her arms in the hope that his love for her could silence her fears, much as his mouth was stifling her protests. He needed to make her understand how he felt. Once she was made to understand his needs, she would surely give herself freely to him . . .

But ultimately Minmei pushed him away and told him in no uncertain terms that he was never to do that again.

Kyle did not understand.

And neither did Rick, who had arrived at the amphitheater in time to witness the kiss but who turned his Battloid around too soon to see the rebuff.

The computer-generated graphics from civil defense command had been patched through to the fortress bridge. A schematic bird's-eye view of the city streets showing the deployment of CD and enemy troops filled the screen of the threat board. Gloval and his crew had been spared actual video footage of the devastating attack, but it didn't take much imagination to visualize the horrors that were befalling the place. These were the streets and landmarks of their world, just as surely as the bridge and base were. Each and every injury inflicted there affected the entire fortress. What happened to one happened to them all.

Gloval was not really a religious man, despite what

his verbal expressions may have suggested. But more than once during the past two years of warfare he'd come close to finding some sort of divine, intervening, benevolent intelligence at work in the cosmos. And most often it had been the Zentraedi's sudden and inexplicable strategic reversals which had given rise to those theological revelations. The captain was in the middle of one of these at the moment, standing stock-still behind Vanessa's chair and staring uncomprehendingly at the novel troop movements on the screen.

"The enemy's actions have become totally chaotic," Vanessa said, stating the obvious.

Gloval nodded his head slowly. "I see it . . . I see it . . . I don't *believe* it, but I see it."

Initially it had appeared that the Zentraedi command was merely relaxing its methodical march and allowing its forces to scatter—to loot or pillage or engage in whatever it was that giants did in Micronian cities. But on closer examination the board revealed that certain pods were chasing, *routing* others. One pod in particular—an Officer's Pod according to its schematic signature—was actually *destroying* them. Gloval let his mind rake quickly over the possibilities: There was Lisa's two-faction theory, a schism in the Zentraedi high command; the chance that some of the VT pilots had for some reason commandeered several pods; and then there was . . . *God*. And perhaps any or all of them spelled God in the end, Gloval decided, as he turned forward to face Lisa and Claudia.

"Alert all auxiliary groups to assemble and lock in on

sectors seven, nine, ten, and eleven. We should be able to box the pods in near the Macross amphitheater." Gloval regarded the board briefly and added, "See if you can raise the Skull team and ascertain their position."

Lisa went to work carrying out the captain's orders. Brown, Indigo, and Green squads were taking up positions near the amphitheater when she finally succeeded in contacting Skull Leader. It had been a long while since Rick had radioed in, and she found herself as relieved as she was angry when he came on-line.

"Uhh, sorry, Commander." He sounded distracted and distant.

"You haven't been reporting in, Rick. Where are you? What's going on?"

"They're here," he answered sadly, turning his head from the cockpit camera. "Kyle and Minmei. Send a rescue group to the amphitheater."

"The amphitheater?" she said in alarm. "Rick, you've got to get them out of there!"

Rick said nothing.

"Have they been hurt, Rick? Answer me. Has something happened to Kyle?"

Lisa saw him reach out for the kill switch, and a second later the monitor screen signals on the bridge went diagonal in static.

Skull One turned its back on the lovers' kiss; dejectedly, the Battloid walked from the amphitheater's tier, head down, arms hanging loosely at its side, interfacing with and mirroring the emotions of its pilot.

Rick felt as devastated as the city itself, at once angry at himself for spying and heartbroken by the result. It had been far worse than that tender cinematic kiss that had riled him so.

How could she have done it? How could she have been so blatantly unfaithful to him?

There wasn't a trace of irony in his inner voice. He desperately *wanted* to feel betrayed, and he meant to put the anger that welled up from the wound to good use.

Max Sterling was waiting for him at the exit gate.

"Did you find her?" Max asked over the net.

"Find who?" Rick spat back.

"Minmei, buddy. Is she in the shelter already?"

Rick almost raised the muzzle of the cannon on his friend.

"She's only one person aboard this ship, Max, you got that? My job is to defend the SDF-1, nothing else."

"Sure," Max said, backing his Battloid away a bit. "Then you'll be happy to learn that you've got your job cut out for you. CD has herded the enemy right into our lap."

Inside the cockpit module Rick stomped on the foot pedals and primed the gatling cannon.

"Then let's go get 'em," he said to Max.

There were eight Battlepods waiting for him on the shattered street and burning rooftops. He acknowledged them with a nod, raised the cannon, screamed a throat-tearing war cry, and launched himself into their midst, skull and crossbones prominently displayed.

The pods poured fire into the street and descended on

him like rabid birds of prey. Running headlong into a horizontal rain of blue death, Rick kept the gatling at waist level, discharging searing fusillades against his ship's enemies. He sustained hits his mind refused to feel and blew away one after another of the galloping pods. Explosions relit the artificial night.

He jagged to the right as one pod took to the air and trap-shot it, two hands on the cannon now and screaming his war cry all the while. He twisted left and blew the legs out from under a second, screen-shot a third. Even when the gatling had expended itself, his blood lust was far from diminished. He went close in, using the cannon as a club; when he lost that, he continued to fight, metal-shod hand to hand.

On the other side of town six pods played dead.

The double-pulled hinged hatch of one these opened, and three small faces peered out. Explosions could still be heard off in the distance, but from the sound of it the fighting was sporadic and winding down. Thanks to Khyron, the Micronians had been able to snatch victory from the very jaws of defeat; their troops were mopping up what the Backstabber's timely escape from the fortress had left unfinished. But the micronized Zentraedi soldiers inside these undamaged spheres had no bones to pick with him. Quite the contrary: *Thanks to Khyron!* indeed.

Rico, Bron, and Konda rappeled to the street on ropes thrown from the cockpit, had they been aware of the Micronian custom, they would surely have kneeled down and offered a kiss. Other Zentraedi began to follow their lead, and soon the entire cult was reunited.

These six pods had managed to keep together since the assault; they had peeled away from the main strike force just before the destruction of the population center had begun. Consequently they had come through the battle relatively unscathed, but most of their fellow deserters had not been as fortunate. Several pods, only a few of them containing micronized Zentraedi, had been unlucky enough to cross paths with Commander Khyron. The diabolical lord of the Botoru Battalion had meted out punishment on the spot. There was no way of guessing just how many soldiers he had put to death; but as word had spread through the ranks, many had given up their hopes for resettlement among the Micronians and fled into space.

As the lucky ones now began to take a look around their dreamland there were mutterings of disappointment and regret. One of their number had found a foot-high Minmei doll on the sidewalk, its embroidered red robe stained and tattered. He was holding it in both hands cheerlessly.

"What's wrong with it?" one of his companions asked. "Why isn't it singing?"

"It seems we've damaged it."

"That doll's not the only thing we've damaged," said Karita, gesturing in general to their surroundings.

"You mean it's not supposed to look like this?"

Bron stepped in and took the doll. "Karita's right. This population center was once beautiful and peaceful."

"The Micronians know how to repair things," Konda added.

"Then they'll rebuild all this?" Karita asked hopefully.

Rico nodded. "They know the secrets of *Protoculture*."

This brought surprised gasps all around, even from those micronized Zentraedi who had no understanding of the word but knew enough to recognize it as the shibboleth of the command elite.

"But what do we do now, Rico? If we're discovered by the Micronians, we'll be executed for our actions against the fortress."

"Yeah, now what?" others chimed in.

Rico thought for a moment. "There's a Micronian who was trying to convince everyone that the war had to be stopped—the one I pointed out to you during the battle record trans-vids we watched. He was talking about peace all the time."

"What's 'peace'?" asked one of the clones, but the others shushed him.

"Go on, Rico."

"Well, I think we should turn ourselves over to the Micronian high command. We'll tell them that we've come in the name of *peace*."

CHAPTER
TWELVE

> *I remember my parents telling me about a popular amusement center that existed before the [Global] War. The place was called EPCOT, and it was located in the southeastern Panam, in what was then called the state of Florida. There you could walk or ride through any number of pavilions, each representative, architecturally and culturally, of its nation of origin. Pop was fascinated by the Mexican exhibit. Apparently, once inside the building, you felt as though you were really in Old Mexico—assuming of course that you were willing to surrender yourself to the imagineers' illusions. A marketplace, an ancient pyramid, even a smoldering volcano—all under a twilight dome full of redolent aromas. Pop was so taken with the pavilion that he went back to it over and over again, and one day he was allowed in before those illusions were in full swing. Much to his later disappointment. Because without that starry sky and that cool and gentle breeze, he was well aware of where he was: inside a human-made environment. The pavilion would never be the same for him again. And this is how the dimensional fortress civilians felt when they left the shelters after the Zentraedi attack. It was all too plain that they were inside an alien spaceship; Macross was changed forever.*
>
> *The Collected Journals of Admiral Rick Hunter*

MAYOR TOMMY LUAN WAS ONE OF THE FIRST TO leave the shelters. He had set out immediately on an inspection tour of Macross that by day's end had left no

proverbial stone unturned. But every step along the way
proved to be an ordeal.

The fires had been extinguished and the thick smoke
exhausted through the enormous exterior ports, but the
air still reeked of molten metals and plastics. The hold
windows and bays, the so-called starlights, were en-
crusted with the same resinous grime that seemed to
have settled on every horizontal surface in the city. The
streets were potholed, cratered, and torn up, running
with water loosed from subsurface and overhead conduits. Recyclable sewage from the devastated oubliette
system had been heaped up here and there or blown into
the air to adhere to street signs and buildings. There
didn't appear to be an intact piece of glass anywhere;
shards littered the sidewalks, the lobbies, the interiors of
offices and homes. In the most unlikely places one was
able to stumble upon pieces of mechanical debris, a car
part here, the leg of a Destroid over there, a Battloid
finger buried in a wall. Perhaps worst of all, there were
those holes in the sky.

Residents were sorting through the mess like zom-
bies, trying to locate fragments of their past lives, staring
shell-shocked at standing walls that no longer embraced
a home, walking eerily to and fro calling out names of
the displaced, the lost, and the dead—of which there
were miraculously few.

For the most part casualties had been confined to the
area around the amphitheater, which had seen the worst
fighting by far. The Star Bowl itself would not house a

concert for a long while, and the surrounding buildings were damaged beyond repair. Here there was hard evidence of the battle: the silent husks of pods and Gladiators still locked together in war-memorial poses, undetonated missiles projecting from storefronts, craters that were in effect immeasurable.

The Macross amphitheater, however, wasn't the only landmark to have been hit. The Hotel Centinel had collapsed like a layer cake, and the neighboring skyway was in shambles. Numerous monorail line pylons had been felled; street and store signs were down. Much of Macross Central Park had burned—the only "living fire" the SDF-1 would ever witness. Electrical power was out in many sections.

Macross was a disaster area.

But Tommy Luan was already rolling up his shirtsleeves and putting things back in order. On the one hand there were several things to be thankful for, he told the populace from a makeshift podium set up on the boulevard not far from the Fortress Theater. The aliens had been beaten back. True, they had leveled quite a bit of the city, but they had not penetrated any of the command areas of the ship—astrogation, engineering, or even the Robotech Defense Forces base. There was certainly an enormous amount of work ahead of them, but they had already rebuilt once before and they would be able to do it again. Luan called on them to think back to a time even earlier than the spacefold accident and recall their experiences during the Global Civil War, when scarcely a city on the planet had escaped devastation in one form or another. Robotechnicians would come to their aid and provide the know-how once again, Luan promised, and Macross would meet those technicians halfway supplying the strength and spirit required to implement their designs. "Rome wasn't built in a day," he reminded them. "Macross City was!"

It was a rousing address, and the city applauded its mayor and spokesperson as much for his determination as for his optimism. There were few among the resident population who doubted that renewal was possible, but an alternative to rebuilding had presented itself to some: Just open the air locks, they publicly maintained. Let space suck out the debris and the memories, and then simply start again from scratch.

For a small and select group of victims the disaster actually facilitated the procurement of much-needed supplies—a different sort of uniform for starters.

"Clothes!" Bron reiterated. "How many times do I have to tell you: Some of the Micronians are soldiers, and some are civilians. The soldiers wear uniforms; the civilians wear clothes. Now repeat it—*clothes*."

"Clothes," said the club members, hangdog expressions on their faces.

"I don't know. . ." Rico said uncertainly. He turned to Konda and Bron for reinforcement. "Can we get away with this?"

The Minmei cultists had abandoned their Battlepods and hiked crosstown—a troop of curious-looking scouts in sackcloth dresses. It had been decided that Rico,

Bron, and Konda would surrender themselves to the SDF-1 high command and explain the reasons for their desertion from the Zentraedi forces. Since the others had little command of the Micronian language, Rico thought it best that they go into hiding for a while. He was actually more concerned about their overeagerness to partake in the Micronian way of life, although he didn't tell them this. All along he'd been proclaiming to have sampled widely of the population center's offerings, and now his followers were beginning to press him for answers he simply didn't have. "When we do get to meet Minmei?" "Can we begin to kiss her immediately?" "How long are we supposed to keep our lips pressed together?" Rico felt like he needed to run off somewhere and hide, but it would probably work out better for everyone if he hid *them* instead.

A hideout would be easy enough to come by, but at some point the micronized soldiers were going to need food. Which meant that one of them was going to have to go out unescorted into the streets. Which meant that clothes were essential. Rico shuddered when he recalled how the Micronians had laughed at Bron when he stepped out in female clothing. Rico shuddered again at the thought of Karita or one of the others stepping out into Micronian society. But *something* had to be done—and *fast*!

Konda, who had the best sense of direction among them, led them through a maze of ruined streets and ultimately into a relatively undamaged department store he remembered from the surveillance visit. The Micronians

were just beginning to emerge from their battle shelters
as they entered the well-stocked store. Rico turned the
group loose and regretted it almost immediately. Karita
and the rest scattered and started stuffing all sorts of
objects into their sackcloth gowns—toys, small appli-
ances, hairbrushes, entertainment discs, time devices,
earlobe ornaments...whatever they could lay their
hands on. It took well over an hour for Rico, Konda, and
Bron to round them up; Karita and a second cultist had
to be forcibly restrained from lip-pressing every fabri-
cated female form they passed.

"Clothes!" Bron shouted angrily when they were all
regrouped. "We're here for clothes and nothing else. Is
that understood?"

Sheepishly they promised to behave and followed
Konda up a stairway (which under normal circumstances
would have been mechanized) and into an area of the
store set apart exclusively for apparel.

"Now, pick what you want and be quick about it!"
Rico yelled as they ran off, their eyes lit up by the display.

Konda was the first to see them return from their
foray: Rico and Bron caught his slack-jawed look and
followed his gaze. Down to the last, they had picked out
female attire—long thin-strapped gowns cut low in front
and back; A-lines and pleated skirts; high-waisted
sleeveless frocks; sweater and skirt ensembles; ruffled
blouses; lingerie, hosiery, and high-heeled shoes.

It took another hour to get everyone properly outfitted, but by the time they left the store there was no rea-

son to doubt they could pass for Micronians. Except, that is, for the three leaders. *Their* next move was to get themselves identified as Zentraedi, and they reasoned that the original sackcloth uniforms might help that along.

The sidewalks and streets were filled with Micronians now, most of whom were busy clearing rubble or sorting through debris. Food and drink booths had been opened for the needy. Armed soldiers and battle mecha patrolled while huge Robotech vehicles hauled away the remains of pods and multigunned civil defense units. The population center was already mobilizing, breaking up into teams and relief groups to deal with the damage. Not fifty paces out of the department store, Rico and the others were assigned to one of these work crews.

At first it looked as though involvement in the detail was going to spell disaster, but Rico's concerns were shortly laid to rest. To the Zentraedi, "repair" was not only a foreign notion but a magical process. Karita and the others had been handed digging devices called shovels and pickaxes and after a few moments of familiarization were completely absorbed in their tasks. They were joyfully swinging and shoveling, shoulder to shoulder with Micronians, even *joining them in song*! It was too perfect, Rico told himself: They would be fed and cared for and looked after. Now, as long as none of them had to speak . . .

With Konda and Bron in tow, Rico managed to weasel out of the area. The three former operatives had far more important things to concern themselves with than clearing debris from the walkways. It was time to turn them-selves in.

Expecting nothing less than complete acceptance and full cooperation, Rico and his cohorts brazenly ap-proached one of the nearby patrol posts and confessed to being Zentraedi agents. But something was wrong; Rico wasn't being taken at his word. The soldier was actually *laughing* at them. So he grew more insistent.

"I'm telling you, we're Zentraedi. We came into the fortress inside one of our battle mecha—"

"You're a little short to be a Zentraedi, aren't you, buddy?" the soldier interrupted.

"We've been through the reduction converter," Bron attempted to explain. "We're micronized."

The soldier exchanged winks with one of his compan-ions.

"'Micronized,' huh? Well, why didn't you say so in the first place?" He put his hand on Rico's shoulder and spun him gently left. "You want that place, right over there. You see, where it says 'medical assistance.'"

"'Medical assistance,'" Rico repeated. "All right, thanks." He turned to Bron and Konda and said, "Come on."

"Shell shock," the lieutenant said to his corporal as the three sackclothed men walked away. "Some kind of martyr thing by the look of it."

At the first-aid station they went through an almost word-for-word repeat performance. But eventually a fe-male wearing a white uniform with a red-cross emblem escorted them into the office of a man who introduced himself as Dr. Zeitgeist.

The room was large and spacious and lined floor to ceiling with archaic document displays. The "doctor" himself was a portly Micronian with an abundance of facial hair but very little on his cranium. He spoke with an accent that made his curious utterances and phrases even more difficult to comprehend. But undaunted, Rico proceeded to recount the details of their desertion from the Zentraedi.

Zeitgeist gave a long "I seeeee..." when Rico finished, and leaned back in his swivel chair. He regarded the three couched men in sackcloths for a moment, then began to review what they'd told him.

"So you three think you're Zentraedi soldiers," said Zeitgeist. (What he actually said was closer to: "Zo you zree zink you're Zentraedi zoldiers." "You were first sent here as spies, but you grew to so love our..." he consulted his notes, "'Micronian' society that you decided to desert your armed forces and live with us."

"Yes, that's it," the three said in unison.

"I seeeee..." said Zeitgeist.

It was the most richly detailed case of guilt-induced Type-Seven behavior that it had been his pleasure to come across in many a day. Certainly a step up from the space phobias, null-g sickness, and separation anxieties he'd been nursing along for the past two years. And so *thorough* and laden with symbolism—from the flagellants' robes to the talk of espionage and "micronization" —that wonderful word which really captured the human sense of displacement one felt inside the alien dimensional fortress. Why he could almost see the journal paper writing itself: "Micronization: The Phobia of Containment."

"And you would ez-timate your actual height," the doctor continued, "to be approx-zimately fifty 'Micronian' feet?"

Rico turned a sober face to Bron and Konda.

"He doesn't believe us."

Bron got to his feet. "We can prove it," he told Zeitgeist. "Bring us to one of your commanders. We'll tell him things about our battle mecha that will convince him."

Over the course of the next few hours the good doctor saw his hopes for a journal paper dashed, but he did begin to think about opening up a counseling clinic for disaffected extraterrestrials. Meanwhile the three Zentraedi were prodded, poked, searched, examined, analyzed, interviewed, tested, scoped, scanned, evaluated, appraised, and assessed. They were moved from office to office, city to cell, and barracks to base. They saw more different types of uniforms than they would have believed existed in the Fourth Quadrant of the known universe. And finally, they were brought before the fortress's commander in chief, Captain Henry Gloval.

Gloval had done little more than browse through the foot-high stack of reports on the debriefing room desk—psychiatric evaluations, intelligence test reports, military and medical examinations, interview transcripts—but he had seen enough to convince him that the aliens' claims were true. What they knew about the workings of the Battlepods alone would have been sufficient evidence. And their very existence in "micronized" size had fully substantiated Lisa's aftermission reports regarding some sort of reduction device aboard the enemy flagship. The clone issue would have to await the results of the medical tests. That these three had actually been in the fortress previously was as amazing as it was discomforting; it was no wonder that Dr. Lang was dying to get his hands on them. First, however, it was up to Gloval and the high command to decide exactly what to do with them. What, in fact, did they want? And how many others like them might be aboard the SDF-1 at this very moment?

These were questions he hoped to have answered before the special session with colonels Maistroff and Caruthers convened.

Lisa Hayes and Max Sterling were now admitted to the room, and shortly thereafter the three aliens were escorted in.

Lisa's first impression erased all doubts that she might have had; in fact, there was almost something *familiar* about these three. Rico put a quick end to her puzzlement.

"We were present at your interrogation," he explained. "Remember when you kissed one of the male members of your group?"

Even though that tidbit had been included in her report, she blushed at hearing about it—from a *Zentraedi*, no less. Rico went on to give details of that meeting with Dolza that were more complete than Rick, Lisa, and

Ben's collective recollection. Then he went on to talk about Breetai and Exedore and someone named Khyron, who had been responsible for turning the tide during the attack on Macross City. The alien also mentioned Proto-culture and Zentraedi fears concerning a Micronian se-cret weapon. They wanted to stay aboard the fortress—this much was clear—and more than anything they wanted to see *Minmei*!

By this time Gloval looked like someone on the verge of sensory overload. His eyes were wide, and his mus-tache was twitching. "That's enough for now," he said, holding up his hands. "We'll carry on with this session in the presence of colonels Maistroff and Caruthers. And Lisa," he added as an aside, "I want you to request that Lieutenant Hunter join us immediately."

CHAPTER
THIRTEEN

When one sits down to a serious side-by-side study of the log entries of the two commanders [Gloval and Breetai], a curious pattern begins to emerge which I believe has been overlooked by many of [the Robotech Wars] commentators and historians . . . And by the time we've reached those entries written just prior to Dolza's direct involvement in the war, this parallel pattern has become self-evident, especially with regard to Lynn-Minmei's importance, the growing disaffection among the ranks, and the defiant stance adopted by both Gloval and Breetai toward their respective high commands (the UEDC and Dolza). It is almost as if two years of space warfare had created what two centuries ago was called a folie à deux.

Rawlins, *Zentraedi Triumvirate: Dolza, Breetai, Khyron*

"**L**IEUTENANT HUNTER'S PRESENCE IS REquested in HQ Special Sessions chamber immediately." No explanation, no afterword, Rick told himself. What, he wondered, had he done now?

There had been no sleep following the battle; the fortress was still on red alert, and all available men and women in the Defense Force were on duty. Most of the tech, engineering, and construction crew had been assigned to Macross, where the civilians had organized work details and clean-up was already under way. Indigo

and Brown VT teams patrolled the city streets in Battloid mode, wary that some Zentraedi might have survived. The SDF-1 was swept stem to stern for infiltration
units, but save for the *Daedalus* arm and the city itself,
there were no signs of enemy penetration. Although casualty counts were not yet complete, there was little
doubt that the losses sustained would number well into
the hundreds, and this didn't take into account a civilian
body count. It would take days to sort through the rubble surrounding the amphitheater alone— a good deal of
which Rick and Max had been responsible for after the
CD squads had successfully stampeded a horde of Battlepods right into their laps.

His blood lust quenched, Rick felt like some sort of
overstimulated incandescent bulb; sleep, even if it was
granted by his superiors, would probably elude him for
weeks. And when that burnout point was finally
reached, it was going to be one heck of a downhill run to
hell . . . He had been ordered to the *Prometheus*, where
he was supervising mecha triage when the request from
Lisa Hayes reached him.

Standing outside the Special Sessions chamber now,
he returned a sentry's salute, tugged at the hem of his
jacket, tried in vain to dewire himself somewhat, and
rapped decisively on the door.

The large room was familiar to him from two other
occasions—when he had been awarded the titanium
Medal of Valor and during his debriefing after imprisonment aboard the Zentraedi flagship. Command would be
seated behind a three-sided continuous desk, somewhat

U-shaped, above which was the winglike Robotech emblem centered in an embossed Defense Forces silver shield. There were bound to be one or two armed sentries positioned on either side of the door, a session transcriber, and of course some hot seat in front of the desk, which Rick hoped had not been reserved for him.

"Lieutenant Hunter reporting as ordered." Rick saluted.

"At ease, Mister Hunter. That was a request, not an order."

Rick wasn't about to relax; he quickly scanned the room. Gloval was seated casually below the shield, elbows on the desk; to his right were Max Sterling and Lisa. On the captain's left, as stiff as ever, were colonels Maistroff and Caruthers, burly veteran commanders both, thick-jowled, tight lipped clones in different color uniforms.

Three men were in the hot seat.

As Rick moved closer, he could see that they were similarly dressed in coarsely woven dark-colored robes. Their strangely unnatural skin tones and hair color varied greatly. And yet there was something familiar about them, something that caught Rick in the pit of his stomach when the three turned around to regard him, something his thoughts and voice refused to make clear but his face betrayed.

"Yes," Captain Gloval said. "These...*men* are aliens."

Rick shook his head. Had Gloval taken leave of his senses? The Zentraedi were giant warriors, *killers*! Their huge body parts and remains were scattered all over Macross City for one and all to see. Rick had seen to that! But even as his mind was shouting all this to his inner ear, an irrefutable realization was fighting its way to the surface.

"B-but *how*?" Rick stammered.

"Apparently those *were* reduction chambers that we saw, Lieutenant Hunter," said Lisa, picking up on his confusion and distress.

"It's pleasant to see you again, Lieutenant," said the gray-faced Zentraedi

"Yes, not long ago you were in a similar position," added the heavy one.

A similar position? Rick asked himself. Then recognition joined realization: These three had been present during the interrogation!

"But what are they doing here, Commander?" Rick held his hands out in a gesture of uncertainty. "Were they captured, or, uh . . ."

"They have come in peace, Hunter."

"Voluntarily and at great personal risk," said Lisa. "They're asking for our protection."

Rick was stunned. "Protection? Are we supposed to say, 'All is forgiven, be my guest,' or what?" He turned to Gloval. "Have you seen Macross, Captain?"

"Relax, Lieutenant."

"Then what do you want from me—my tacit approval?"

"You're here for the same reason that I asked Commander Hayes and Lieutenant Sterling to join us: because you've had prior contact with the aliens."

Rick turned to the aliens. They were pressed together on the hot seat couch, expectant, almost jubilant looks on their faces.

"Why? What are your reasons for deserting, for wanting to join us? You don't know anything about us."

"We want to live the Micronian life," said Bron.

"There is happiness aboard this ship," said Konda.

"Minmei is here," said Rico.

Rick was speechless. Did the alien really say "Minmei" or had he just imagined it? All of a sudden he felt nauseous. His voice sounded thin and strained as he asked them how they knew about Micronian ways and . . . *Minmei*. And their answer was even more surprising than he had feared.

"We have already lived among you as spies."

For Rick's benefit the captain recapped what had been learned in previous debriefing sessions with the aliens. How they had been inserted into the SDF-1 at the same time Lisa and Rick's Vermilion Team had made their great escape; how the three agents had walked unnoticed for weeks through Macross City; how they had made their own great escape from Bird Island; how tales of their exploits and disaffection with war had spread through the Zentraedi fleet; how there were more than a dozen others like them aboard the fortress even now; and how Minmei was at the center of it all.

". . . And the most beautiful things of all were Minmei's singing and the fact that males and females, er, stayed together."

"Some people even spoke out against fighting," Rico added.

Kyle! Rick said to himself.

"Once we became used to it," Konda was saying, "we started to like living here."

"We can't go back," Bron reminded them.

"And what would be the sense, since it is known that you control the Protoculture."

All heads turned to purple-haired Konda.

"Exactly what is this 'Protoculture'?" asked Caruthers, speaking for the first time since Rick's entrance.

"You know exactly what it is," Bron said flatly.

"It's not nice to make fun of us."

Rico seemed to be sincere about it, but Gloval wanted to avoid the issue of Protoculture during this first session. He cleared his throat and asked Rick how he would feel about granting the aliens political asylum.

Rick had sensed it coming for a while and had been slowly formulating his thoughts. "I would be in favor of it," he told the panel. "If only as a first step toward a possible truce or peace." There was no need to mention the obvious military advantages to be gained once the aliens had been fully debriefed.

"I can't believe what I'm hearing," said Caruthers. "Just a moment ago you were reminding us of the atrocities that these . . . *creatures* had perpetrated on Macross, and now you're willing to grant them asylum."

"Really, Captain Gloval," Maistroff added, picking up

the ball. "Don't you think we should be consulting with someone who has a clearer understanding of this entire matter? I, for one, am not convinced of their claims. This is a ruse."

"Hmmm," Gloval mused. "Anything you want to add, Hunter?"

Rick faced the colonels. "The aliens are bred for war and conquest. It's the only life they've known. But contact with our ways has erased who knows how many generations of aggressive conditioning almost overnight. Singing, marriage, love. Even a kiss can set them off— Commander Hayes and I indicated that much in our report.

"There has to be some attempt made at peace."

"Good lord, man!" said Caruthers, his fist striking the desktop. "You're talking about living with *aliens*!"

Maistroff mirrored the gesture. "They may *look* like us, Lieutenant Hunter, but don't be fooled: I'm certain that this is some sort of Zentraedi trap."

"You weren't aboard that Zentraedi cruiser, Colonel. I'm telling you, these three had their first taste of freedom aboard the SDF-1, and the word has already started to spread. By granting them asylum we're demonstrating that ours is the better life. We can create a mutiny in that fleet."

"If three are willing to desert," said Lisa, "three hundred will, then three thousand."

Caruthers laughed shortly. "Now, there's some nice emotional logic."

"We must make them understand that there are alternatives to war," Lisa continued. "If we can get them to understand another way of life, one that's not a matter of win or die, maybe we can change the focus of their lives and live with them in peace."

"Very eloquent," said Maistroff, applauding, his voice dripping sarcasm. "A truly excellent speech, Commander Hayes. But these are *aliens* we're dealing with. You can't possibly expect them to adapt to our way of life."

The three still-couched Zentraedi were turning their heads from speaker to speaker, trying to follow the conversation. Frowns of concern had replaced their initially confident expressions. Rico was about to say something, but just then someone knocked at the doorway and entered the Special Sessions room unannounced. It was one of Lang's white-frocked, glassy-eyed Robotechnicians.

"What is the meaning of this?" demanded Caruthers. "How dare you barge in like this?"

The man was carrying a file which he presented straightaway to Gloval, undaunted by Caruthers's reprimand. The captain returned a salute and aimed a dismissive gesture toward the colonel. "I asked Lang to have this sent to me as quickly as possible."

Gloval began to run through the file, uttering sounds of interest and surprise.

Max, Lisa, and Rick exchanged glances.

"What's he got there?" Sterling whispered.

"Lang's medical profiles on the aliens," Lisa returned.

The colonels were halfway out of their chairs peering at the file. "Well, what is it, Captain?" Maistroff asked at last.

Gloval passed him the file. "I had the laboratory analyze the aliens' cell structure. You may find this intriguing. As a matter of fact, I'm certain you will."

Save for the sound of pages being turned, the room was silent while Maistroff and Caruthers read. Ultimately the file began to shake in the colonel's hands.

"It's incredible! Why, their blood types and genetic structures are virtually identical to ours! We're effectively the same beings!"

This seemed to shock the three Zentraedi as much as anyone else in the room.

"I expected something like this," Lisa remarked.

"You could be right, Commander," said Max. "We might have a common ancestor race, after all."

"Well now, it seems to me that we can no longer treat these, ah, *people* as aliens. I believe we're safe in proceeding with this case as we would with any other request for political asylum."

"Hold on a minute, Gloval," Maistroff protested. "First of all, I don't think that the results of one lab test should influence the decisions of this council. As far as I'm concerned, Lang's evidence is inconclusive. Lord knows the man has reason enough to want to keep these three aboard. But that's beside the point. And so what if we *are* of similar genetic background? These men—and I use the term advisedly—are the enemies of this ship and all aboard her. I move for imprisonment until such time as their true purpose for being here can be ascertained."

Gloval listened closely, nodding his head, then said, "And as captain of this vessel, I say we grant these gentlemen political asylum."

The three Zentraedi were on their feet hugging each other even before the last word left the captain's mouth. Rick, Lisa, and Max risked guarded smiles. But Maistroff was enraged, standing at his chair and pounding the desk with his fist.

"We can't make a decision as important as this without first consulting the United Earth Defense Council!"

"You better hear him, *Captain*," Caruthers was saying.

"I accept the responsibility," Gloval answered them firmly.

Red-faced, Maistroff swallowed whatever it was he was going to say. He motioned to Caruthers that they should leave, but at the door he turned and promised: "You haven't heard the end of this, Gloval."

"Captain," Lisa said after a moment.

Gloval acknowledged her.

"We're going to have trouble with them. They won't let it go at this. They'll make contact with Earth HQ and try to get your decision overturned."

Gloval turned a weary face to all of them. "We are forced to take extraordinary measures. If the Earth Council wishes to continue denying the facts, then so be it. But aboard this ship *I* will decide. Let them doom themselves if they wish, but they will no longer sit in judgment of our fate."

CHAPTER
FOURTEEN

"Rick, I'm going out of my head," [Max Sterling] would say to me. "I've been searching the city since I saw her at the premiere, and no one seems to know her or know where she lives. I mean, how can that be? I thought everybody knew everybody in Macross! I swear I'm in love with her; I'm going to ask her to marry me if I ever see her again!" . . . And I remember saying to him, "Sterling, you're going to marry a girl with green hair?" It was a foolish enough remark given the fact that Max had worn a blue tint in his hair ever since I'd known him, but an absolute riot considering who Miriya turned out to be!

The Collected Journals of Admiral Rick Hunter

QUADRONO ACE MIRIYA PARINO DID A DOUBLE take as the Micronian work crew passed her on Macross Boulevard. It wasn't the big smile on the foreman's face that caught her attention—she was used to those appraising looks by now—but the equally silly faces of a group of stragglers who seemed to have attached themselves to this particular crew. This whistling happy-go-lucky subgroup of males—there must have been ten of them—carried their shovels and crude digging implements as if they were sacred relics, and the ear-to-ear grins they wore (not directed toward Miriya, in any case) appeared to radiate from some newfound inner sense of wonder and exuberance. This in itself was not uncommon among the Micronians, even in the midst of all the present devastation, but there was something about the posturing and enthusiasm that led Miriya to believe things were not entirely as they seemed.

She began to follow them along a course that wound its way through the devastated city streets, across planks that spanned battle-created craters, through the burned-out hulks of houses and buildings, around carefully organized and sorted piles of debris and the slag-heap remains of ruined mecha, and finally into the heavily damaged amphitheater, where the workers began an assault on the rubble. Assisted by massive Robotech droids and processors, the men and women threw themselves into the task with an unmatched display of discipline and commitment. The stragglers were no exception to this. But as Miriya moved in for a closer look, she recognized one of them: It was *Karita*—the Zentraedi officer assigned to the sizing chambers aboard Commander Breetai's flagship! Even those finely tailored Micronian trousers and that cardigan sweater could not disguise him.

As Miriya began to look around, she recognized several others from Breetai's ship and instantly realized what was going on. She had to congratulate the Commander on a brilliant plan. Obviously the Zentraedi attack against the population center was more in the way of a diversionary action. The actual purpose of the raid was to see to it that a sizable contingent of micronized agents would be inserted into the dimensional fortress. Their mission was to infiltrate the work crews and attain firsthand knowledge of the Protocultural process that enabled the Micronians to effect repairs to their damaged Robotechnological devices—information long withheld from the Zentraedi by their Robotech Masters but something Zor would have wanted them to possess.

Miriya was content, she would be able to return to her own mission without having to concern herself with the progress of the war. Breetai was doing his part, Miriya, hers.

She left the amphitheater, pushing her way through throngs of busy Micronians, deliberately stepping between male-female couples whenever she had the opportunity.

Miriya was on her way to one of the fighter pilots' training centers—at least that was what she reasoned it to be. VIDEO ARCADE, she read above the doorway. Whatever that meant. Inside were two floors of electronic fighter-training devices for young Micronians. It was no wonder the so-called VT pilots were so adept at handling their mecha; they were trained from infancy to fly and fight. Several of the training devices were even designed to perpetuate archaic hand-to-hand combat techniques. Miriya had become fascinated by one of these in particular, a device called "Knife-Fight." It was possible that when the time came for Miriya to face off with her Micronian archenemy, there would be no battle mecha available. She therefore planned to prepare herself for any and all eventualities.

"What are you looking at, Rick?"

"That girl," he started to say.

"She was pretty rude if you ask me, pushing between us like that when she could just as easily have stepped to the side."

"Yeah, but that green hair..."

"You find that attractive?"

"No...no, of course not, Lisa. It's just that Max has been looking all over for some green-haired girl, and that might be her."

"Tell Max she's rude."

"Yeah, sure, but did you see where she went?"

"I really wasn't looking, Rick."

"Must've turned off into one of those stores, maybe the arcade."

"Do you want to stop and look for her or what?"

"Huh? No, no way. I'll just let Max know that I saw her."

"You do that."

They were on a walking tour of the damage; no particular place to go. People were scrambling around getting things done, taking care of business, fixing this and that. "Public works," one of Rick's more cynical VT friends had said, "keeps their minds off the war."

"Is it like this all over?" Lisa asked, wanting to change the subject.

Rick nodded. "Nearly every part of the city was damaged in the attack."

"I wonder what the casualty figures will be like."

"I don't know," said Rick. And he didn't want to know.

Eventually their wanderings brought them around to the White Dragon. (*Let Rick have the lead and you always seem to end up here*, Lisa told herself.) The building itself looked untouched, but an overturned delivery van was still smoldering in the street. There were enormous breaches in the overhead tier in this section—jagged holes and lightning fissures. Uncle Max and his wife Lena, Macross City's oddest couple, were just exiting from the hexagonally shaped doorway. Rick called out to them and broke into a run.

"Rick!" said Max. "What in the world are you doing here? Are you all right?"

"I'm fine, but what about you? Where are you two off to?"

"We've been worried sick about Kyle and Minmei," said Aunt Lena. "We heard that the Star Bowl was practically destroyed, and I just can't stand waiting around here any longer, praying they'll show up."

Max took his wife's hand and gave it a reassuring squeeze.

"They're at the hospital," Rick told them. "But there's no need to worry; they're both fine."

"Oh, thank God!" said Lena.

"Kyle is bruised up, and Minmei just went along to hold, ah, look after him, see that he was all right."

"Do you think we'd be allowed to see them, Rick?"

"It's a bit of a mess over there right now," said Lisa. "But they'll let you through, I'm certain of it."

Rick suggested that they give it a try and spontaneously volunteered to keep an eye on the restaurant during their absence. Lisa agreed, and Rick's surrogate family hurried off.

Inside, they had their work cut out for them. Large portions of water-damaged gypsum board had collapsed from the ceiling; water dripped from a broken overhead pipe. Tables and chairs were overturned; pictures had fallen from the walls; the remains of dishes and glassware shaken from cabinets littered the floor. On every horizontal surface from the smallest ledge to the only still-standing table was a gritty black coating of resinous ash. Ultimately the entire place was going to need a couple of coats of paint, but until then they could at least take care of the custodial chores—cleaning, sweeping, scrubbing.

Rick opted for the shovel and broom detail while Lisa attacked the tables and chairs with a detergent fluid. Rick noticed that she hummed to herself while she worked. It brought a smile to his face each time she stepped from behind that commander's mask. Here she was being *domestic*... Here *he* was being domestic! And he actually felt good, just losing himself in the mindlessness of it and seeing immediate results for a change. There was a beginning and an end to this task.

Two hours later the mess had been cleared, the tables and chairs uprighted.

"You know what would be good right now, Rick? A cup of fresh tea. I'll do the honors."

Rick said, "Be my guest," and walked over to straighten one last picture. It was a framed photo of Minmei taken over a year ago, sometime after the Miss Macross pageant. He reached out a gloved hand and tipped it back to vertical, the harsh memory of that stage kiss replaying itself as he did so, a continuous loop that time and endless viewing had yet to erase. *It's over now*, he was saying to himself when Lisa entered from the kitchen with two cups.

I've lost her to stage, screen, Kyle, and now to the enemy!

"Don't burn yourself," she warned him.

They sat at one of the tables overlooking the street. Work crews had moved into the area to cart off debris and undertake floor-by-floor searches of each building. Lisa watched a group of strange-looking men busy themselves clearing rubble as she sipped her tea. They seemed downright *enthusiastic*, and it got her to thinking.

"You know, Rick, these simple activities don't mean much to us, but to the Zentraedi our everyday, humdrum world must seem wonderful by comparison. It doesn't surprise me at all that Rico and those other two decided to defect. Sometimes I think *I'd* like to desert. Just forget about the military and get myself back to basics." She laughed to herself. "Get myself *back*. Listen to me. I've never even *been* there."

"Are you thinking about the Zentraedi or Kyle?" Rick asked smugly.

She grinned wryly. "It's a pipe dream, and I know it. I'm Ms. Military, and he hates the military. Great way to begin a relationship, right? But it's true that I've been nursing some doubts since I met him. He's a ghost who's come back to haunt me. Everything about him: his looks, all his antiwar speeches. I keep seeing Karl. And it doesn't help any when we've got to hear Maistroff and Caruthers expressing the same old . . . you know what I'm talking about."

"So much for playing it by the book, huh?"

"Who knows? And as for Lynn-Kyle, he doesn't know I exist. I've got two strikes against me: this uniform and Minmei." She saw Rick's face grow long and apologized.

"If you don't want to talk about it . . ."

"There's nothing to talk *about*." Rick turned his face away. "I'm angrier at myself than I am with her. I mean, how could I have been so *sure* that we had something together when as far as she was concerned we were just friends? Someday you'll have to get me drunk and I'll tell you all about our wonderful two weeks together in the basement of this ship."

"I'm a good listener, Rick. I'm not going to judge you or anything."

He shook his head. "Maybe some other time. I'm just sick of getting all twisted up by the whole thing. Let her stay with her cousin. Let her marry him for all I care. I just wanna have all this behind me for a change. It's really *bizarre*, and that's the long and short of it. Back on Earth I could at least move to another town or another country. But we're all stuck on the ship for the duration, the whole nine yards. Just one big happy family of space wanderers."

He had tears in his eyes when he looked at Lisa again, but his voice was self-mocking. "This was probably how it was at the beginning, a few thousand hominids running around the Serengeti and every one of them in love with the wrong person."

Lisa laughed and covered her mouth with her hand.

"I think you're writing yourself off too soon, Rick. Maybe it'll just take time. Have you ever actually told her how you feel?"

Rick shrugged. "My actions speak for me."

"Not enough. Sometimes it's just not enough. You have to tell her. Otherwise, she's in the dark and Kyle *will* take her away. Of course, you'll get to hold on to your regrets and your self-pity..."

Lisa recalled Claudia telling her as much.

"Is that what I'm doing? Is that how you really see it?" His watery eyes were locked on hers, searching.

She exhaled slowly.

And a warning siren went off outside.

"Another attack!" said Lisa, jumping up from the table. "You better get back to the base! I'll lock up in here and meet you at the rail line!"

"Don't take too long," he told her from the doorway. "Sammie can't handle your station!"

"Be careful!" she called after him, but he was already gone.

"Enemy battle mecha," said Claudia Grant. "Course heading zero-zero-niner, Third Quadrant. Looks like the same group to me, Captain."

Gloval agreed with her assessment after studying the readout. The same two dozen Zentraedi pods and fighters had appeared on the threat board after the attack on Macross, moving erratically from quadrant to quadrant, half the time in pursuit of the fortress and at other times speeding from it. There was reason to believe that these were the very ships that had escaped from the fortress after the CD forces had gained the upper hand. Perhaps, Gloval now speculated, under the command of this apparently crazed Zentraedi officer named Khyron, whom the three defectors had mentioned over and over, sometimes referring to him as "the Backstabber." Rico had actually credited him with more Battlepod kills than the combined total of the Defense Forces.

"Skull Team is up and away, Captain," Gloval heard Sammie report from Lisa's station. He noticed that her foot was tapping nervously. "Kirkland," she continued, "prepare to supply cover. They'll be coming about on your right flank."

"*Left* flank," Claudia corrected her. "Their cat's away from *Prometheus*."

"Uh, scratch that, Kirkland. Look for Delta on your left flank. Indigo, your signal is 'buster.' Return to base immediately. Uh, uh...*Damn it!* Where is Commander Hayes? I'm going crazy—"

"Right behind you, Sammie," Lisa said breathlessly. She turned a quick salute to the captain: "Sorry I was delayed, sir."

"It's all yours," Sammie said, stepping aside.

"Estimate five minutes to contact," said Vanessa.

Gloval glanced over at the board. The Zentraedi warships were still holding at their postattack coordinates. What could this small contingent of pods have in mind?

"Looks like a kamikaze run," said Claudia. "They should know better than that by now."

Lisa turned to her. "Judging from what the defectors had to say, I wouldn't put it past them to try anything from now on." She raised Skull Leader on the net. "Bandits will be in your lap in three minutes, Lieutenant."

"Roger," Rick answered her. "I show them on wide beam."

"Try telling them to go home, Lieutenant Hunter."

Rick's laugh came through the speaker, followed by a loud and seemingly sincere, "Go home!"

Still unwilling to rule out miracles, Lisa checked the displays.

"Uh, sorry, Skull Leader. Nice try, but it didn't work."

"I copy that, Commander. Guess we've gotta speak to them in the only language they understand."

Lisa's screen began to light up; the enemy mecha had

opened fire. Skull and the other teams were engaging them. Radar blips began to disappear from the board, VTs and enemy paint.

"Never say die, Rick," she said softly into her mike.

CHAPTER
FIFTEEN

...But if such a contest existed, I would cast my vote without hesitation for Khyron—history's principal man in the middle. Distrusted by Dolza, dismissed by Breetai, feared by his own troops, and now fixed upon by the "Micronians," Khyron had moved into what might be called transparanoia (or better still, metanoia). He simply was all those things normal paranoid personality types delude themselves into believing: persecuted, grandiose, and essentially pivotal in the great scheme of things.

Rawlins, *Zentraedi Triumvirate:
Dolza, Breetai, Khyron*

THE ZENTRAEDI FLAGSHIP HAD SELF-SEALED ITSELF; an undetectable patch of green armor covered the damage done to its blunt nose by the ramming arm of the fortress—a design feature the Robotech Masters had engineered into the ships of the fleet. Would that breaches in command were so easily sealed, thought Breetai, and breaches in discipline.

Just now he was pacing the floor of the observation booth, as always, under the analytical gaze of his misshapen adviser.

Though limited in emotional range, the Zentraedi commander had run the gamut of available responses since the inception of Exedore's plan to assault the SDF-1 right through to Khyron's news of mass desertion among the ranks. Things had looked good early on: He had forced the Micronians to launch their so-called *Daedalus* Maneuver, their Destroids had been destroyed, and Regault squads of Battlepods had been successfully inserted into the fortress. There were indications of a massive battle having taken place in the population center inside the Robotech ship; the Micronians had recalled most of their fighters to deal with the threat, and follow-up transmissions on the tac net suggested that the Zentraedi had scored a decisive victory. Much to Breetai and Exedore's surprise, Khyron's Botoru teams had also infiltrated the enemy's defense. Breetai had grown confident of a sure Micronian surrender. Zor's Protoculture matrix would soon be his, and with it would come greater glory than any had hitherto known.

But then word had been received from Khyron about the desertions.

Breetai refused to believe it.

"This must be the tremendous force the Robotech Masters have been speaking of," Exedore said. "The legends have been most specific: Continued contact with Micronians is to be avoided at all costs. They are said to be in possession of a secret weapon which could ultimately destroy us, leaving this quadrant wide open for an attack by the Invid. I have long dreaded this day, m'lord."

Breetai expected no less; his advisor had been quoting the legends to him since that first day when the fleet defolded from hyperspace near the Micronians' homeworld.

"So you think I should have paid attention to those ancient warnings, do you?"

"Perhaps, m'lord."

"And what of Commander in Chief Dolza, Exedore? What would we do about him?"

"The question remains not what we *would* have done, Commander," Exedore countered, "but what we *will* do about him."

Desertion had turned the battle around. Although Breetai had yet to formulate a clear picture of the events, Commander Khyron reported that he had been forced to take punitive measures against some of the Zentraedi troops. Soldiers had been abandoning their mecha and expressing a wish to live among the Micronians. Some sort of psychological assault had been launched against them—Khyron said that the deserters had referred to it as a "Minmei." Obviously the perfected form of the weapon the Micronians had been experimenting with for at least a year by their own reckoning. Breetai recalled those early days: the low-frequency transmissions from the fortress which had so confused Exedore's three Cyclops operatives, and later, the disturbing effects produced by the male and female captives. Subsequently there was the strange behavior of the returned spies and the trans-vids of that Micronian battle record and death ray demonstration.

The secrets of Protoculture were theirs!

Driven from the dimensional fortress, Khyron had since been pursuing a group of potential deserters, dispatching them one by one. He now had them regrouped and headed again toward the SDF-1 on a suicide run. Breetai, however, was having second thoughts: It was too late to undo any of his past mistakes, but he might yet be able to profit from this latest upset. Commander Azonia had informed him that Quadrono leader Miriya was still aboard the fortress. Surely she'd see to it that the deserters wouldn't live long enough to do the Zentraedi any harm. And as for these few stragglers . . .

"Tell Khyron to call off his attack," Breetai now told his advisor. "We will remove all our troops from Micronian influence immediately."

Exedore bowed slightly. "And then, m'lord?"

"Interrogate the deserters. You must see if you can determine the nature of this power the Micronians have exerted. We may yet find a way to resist their control."

"It shall be done."

Khyron had centered one of the Battlepods in his targeting screen. It would require only a glancing blow to the upper right of the sphere to bring the thing back into line. Mustn't let them stray too far from the fold, he said to himself. *All Micronian sympathizers have to stick together.* He was just elevating one of the mecha's handguns and bringing it to bear on the pod when Exedore raised him on the comlink.

Breetai's orders were relayed.

"Isolate the deserters and lock them up?!" Khyron shouted into his communicator. "Exedore, are you mad? What next, if we let them get away with this?"

"You have your orders, Commander."

Khyron slammed his fist down on the control console of the Officer's Pod. "We might just as well surrender to the Micronians!"

"Order your troops about, Commander. Commander Breetai has ordered me to employ the nebulizer if you fail to comply."

"And what about the deserters aboard that ship?" Khyron demanded. "Do you realize what damage they can do?"

"Miriya will see to them, Commander."

Khyron was stunned. "Miriya? Miriya Parino is aboard—*micronized*?! Why wasn't I informed of this?"

"That is Commander Breetai's prerogative," Exedore said plainly.

"Bah!"

Khyron shut down the comlink. So this was how it was going to be, he said to himself. New lines were being drawn. And sooner or later he and Breetai were going to find themselves on opposite sides. A sinister smile began to surface. Let Breetai have his deserters, the infected ones. The illness would spread through his fleet like an epidemic, and Dolza would hear about it. With both Azonia and Breetai out of the way, Khyron would be put in command. Then the real purge would commence; and not just against the Micronians but against *all* those who defied the Zentraedi imperative!

Human and Zentraedi mecha met head-on, crisscrossing silently in space at skirmish speed. The Veritechs held back their fire until the last possible moment, then unleashed a storm of missiles and gatling rounds at the Battlepods and triple-fins. Spherical explosions threw short-lived light against the night. Below them was the dark face of the Earth, undisturbed and unconcerned.

Skull One's retros flared briefly to bleed the fighter of velocity as ventral thrusters provided its lift, tipping the ship over so that Earth was now above Rick for a moment. Most of the pods had also doubled back but had yet to return fire. VTs from Vermilion and Blue teams were blowing them out of space like sitting ducks. And where Lisa had been expecting a kamikazelike attack, there was only a full-scale retreat. Rick moved to within striking distance of two ostriches, his front fuselage guns blazing, but the enemy refused to engage him; they simply rolled and showed him the red glow of their foot thrusters.

"Certain reluctance out here or am I imagining things?" said Vermilion Leader over the tac net.

"I copy that, V Leader," someone added.

"Skull One, do we pursue?"

"Uh, affirmative, V Leader," said Rick. "Let's go see what they're up to."

The Veritechs regrouped and boostered off after the fleeing Battlepods. Rick was the first to spot the Officer's Pod; it seemed to be taking aim at one of its own, herding the mecha back into formation with the rest. Rick hit his afterburners and homed in on it.

He couldn't hold the enemy officer in the reticle but had a good view of the ship on his forward scopes. It had to be the same one! Rick convinced himself. There were no telltale markings of any kind—it was easily as worn, scorched, and scratched as the rest of them—but that pilot seemed to have his own signature. And from what the defectors had divulged, the name attached to that craft would be "Khyron"—someone they seemed to fear above all else.

Rick noticed two VTs from Blue making their approach against the Officer's Pod. But Khyron was alert to their scheme and went after them in a frenzy, handguns blasting away, top-mounted cannon erupting in salvos of death. Both Veritechs sustained hits and disintegrated in the ensuing explosions.

Meanwhile Rick was certain he had the drop on the pod. Distracted by the two fighters, his quarry had turned his back to him, all guns forward. But as Skull One sped in for the shot, the pod swiveled and caught sight of him. Rick launched three missiles regardless, but pulsed bombardment detonated the first, and the second and third fell to fratricide.

The tables were turned all of a sudden. The pod had a good opportunity to tail Rick and slide easily into position for that lethal cone release, but in the interim, Khyron's charges had escaped his control. So instead of jumping on Rick, the pod turned around to reshepherd its widespread flock.

"They seem to be breaking off for good, Lieutenant," said the Vermilion Leader.

Rick breathed a sigh of relief before he went on the net. "Have your teams pull back to the fortress." He then raised Max on the commo screen.

"Scanners show warships along our heading, Skull One."

"All right, Max. Looks like they decided to go home, after all. Let's do the same."

One by one the Veritechs retroed and began to reverse their headings. The SDF-1, reconfigured to Cruiser mode now, was waiting for them in the space above Earth's sunny side.

Later, Lisa met with Captain Gloval in his quarters. Ever since colonels Maistroff and Caruthers had walked out on the asylum session, she had been searching for some way to counteract their influence with the United Earth Defense Council. Should the UEDC leaders overturn Gloval's ruling, there was no telling what might become of the defectors. For all anyone aboard the SDF-1 knew, Rico and his companions could possess some means of spreading the word, good or bad, back to the Zentraedi fleet. They had stated that there were ten other micronized soldiers in hiding. And perhaps those ten were prepared to engage in acts of sabotage if asylum was refused. Things hadn't gone very well with her father the last time they met, but surely he would have to be open-minded now, in light of these recent developments and this new physical evidence of a possible link between Humans and Zentraedi. She told Gloval as much.

"You know I'm right, sir. When we granted asylum to those defectors, we changed this whole conflict. We're defending their desire to adopt our values. If I don't go to Earth and line up some support, we might very well be ordered to send them back."

Gloval had his back to her while he listened. But now he swung away from the starfield view out the portside bay and faced her. He was skeptical.

"Our dealings with the Council have proved less than satisfying so far. What makes you think you'll be able to convince them now?"

"I'm not *promising* anything, Captain. But we do have new evidence on our side. If I can just get my father behind us."

"That's a very large *if*, Lisa."

"The results of Dr. Lang's lab tests should be enough to reopen a dialogue with the Council if nothing else. The Zentraedi race and the Human race are essentially the same. They could be our long-lost brothers and sisters. If that isn't compelling enough, I don't know what is."

"You're determined to make this work."

"Yes, sir. I'm aware of what you said after the session—that you're no longer going to let the council dictate to this ship—but I would hate to see things go in that direction. No matter how disaffected the civilians are, Macross will never be the same after that attack.

They have to be disembarked and resettled on Earth. What can we do otherwise? Search the galaxy for some hospitable world? If we still had our fold generators that might be possible, but given the speeds we can attain . . . I don't have to tell you this, Captain."

Gloval waved his hand dismissively. "You're right to say it. I need to hear it sometimes."

Lisa perched herself on the corner of his desk. "We've been lucky. But how much longer can this go on? Even if the Zentraedi never achieve a decisive victory, they're going to succeed in whittling us down to nothing. Our stores are not inexhaustible. And God knows, our Defense Force isn't inexhaustible. And no matter what the Council proclaims—no matter what they threaten us with—this ship is *not* expendable. We are the only thing that stands between the Zentraedi armada and the Earth itself." Lisa motioned out the bay to the stars. "They have over one *million* warships out there! We're losing sight of that because we've been lucky and they've been foolish. But even in the best of winning streaks luck has an uncanny way of reversing itself. We have to come to terms with the Council and the Zentraedi. I think the appearance of the defectors is the first step in that process, and *they* took it. Maybe we've already done our part by offering asylum, but I'm convinced we have to go further. I've got to get to my father before Maistroff and Caruthers get to him."

Gloval tugged at his mustache. "It could be risky, Lisa."

"How, sir?"

"Because your father wants you off this ship. And if we lose you now..."

She smiled at him. "You have Sammie, Captain. She'll get the hang of it."

Gloval snorted. "Sammie will someday make a proper First Officer, but she lacks your overall knowledge of this fortress. You are needed here, Lisa."

"Thank you, sir," she said, lowering her gaze. "But this war *must* be stopped. Let me try this approach, Captain. I promise you I won't let my father prevent my return."

Gloval nodded and exhaled loudly. "All right, you have my permission. But think carefully before you decide to disobey any orders from the Council. Remember who and what you are, Lisa."

She stood up sharply and saluted him. "I'll begin working on a joint report tonight and have a draft for you in the morning."

Gloval stood up and extended his hand to her. "You'll leave as soon as possible."

Lisa was already formulating her report when she left the captain's quarters, experimenting with wording and editing, choosing the phrases and approach that would work best with her father. She was so wrapped up in this process that she got halfway to the bridge before realizing that she was supposed to be headed to her barracks. Turning around, she became preoccupied with a different train of thought: It was possible that she might never set foot on the bridge again. Captain Gloval was right; her father wanted her off the SDF-1, and he would try to make good his demands this time—especially after hearing the news she was bringing. She could hear him now: *What?! Aliens aboard the fortress?! A-and Gloval's granted them political asylum? A-and you expect me to allow you to return to that ship of fools?!*

This started her thinking along a line of "last thoughts": This might be the last time she walked this corridor, the last time she slept in her quarters, the last time she saw her crewmates—Claudia, Sammie, Kim, Vanessa . . . and Rick. What would Rick say if he knew she was leaving?

Had Lisa walked directly to the elevator, she would have had an opportunity to ask him in person, because the lieutenant had stepped off a moment before she arrived. And it would have been doubly interesting considering that he had been wondering how she might react to his asking her out to dinner.

But fate operated along the same lines then as it does today, and her autopilot wrong turn along the corridor had erased all chance of a meeting. Dinner would have to wait—for quite a while if the truth be permitted at this stage of the narrative. And not onboard the SDF-1, either. Events were about to take a twist everyone had feared but no one had dared anticipate. The war was about to escalate. Death was about to gain the upper hand. Rick and Lisa *would* meet again, but against a landscape that would overshadow any joy such a reunion might ordinarily bring.

The following chapter is a sneak preview of *Force of Arms*—Book V in the continuing saga of ROBOTECH!!

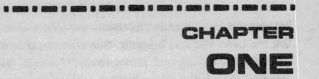

"YA AIN'T SO BIG NOW, ARE YA, YA FREAKIN'
alien?" the big bruiser said, shaking a big scarred fist in
his face.

Well, no, he wasn't. Karita *had* been a Zentraedi soldier some fifty feet tall. But now, having been reduced to
the size of a Human and defecting to their side in the
Robotech War, he was only a medium-build, slightly
less-than-average-height fellow facing three hulking
brawlers eager to split his head wide open in a Macross
alley.

Even as a Zentraedi, Karita hadn't excelled at combat; his main duty had been tending the sizing chambers, the very same ones in which he had been micronized. The situation looked hopeless; the three ringed him in, fists cocked, light from the distant street lamps illuminating the hatred in their faces.

He tried to dodge past them, but they were too fast. The biggest grabbed him and hurled him against the wall. Karita dropped, half-stunned, the back of his scalp bleeding.

He cursed himself for his carelessness; a slip of the tongue in the restaurant had given him away. Otherwise, no one could have told him apart from any other occupant of the SDF-1.

But he could scarcely be blamed. The wonders of life aboard the super dimensional fortress were enough to make any Zentraedi careless. The Humans had rebuilt their city; they mingled, both sexes, all ages. They lived lives in which emotions were given free expression, and there was an astonishing force called "love."

It was enough to make any Zentraedi, born into a Spartan, merciless warrior culture with strict segregation of the sexes, forget himself. And so Karita had made his error; he had gone into the White Dragon in the hopes of getting a glimpse of Minmei. He didn't realize what he was saying when he let slip the fact that he'd adored her since he had first seen her image on a Zentraedi battlecruiser. Then he saw the hard looks the trio gave him. He left quickly, but they followed.

During the course of the war, everybody aboard the dimensional fortress had lost at least one friend or loved one. The Zentraedi, too, had suffered losses—many more than the SDF-1, in fact. That didn't stop Karita and the others from hoping for a new life among their former enemies. Most Humans were at least tolerant of the Zentraedi who'd defected from their invading armada. Some Humans even *liked* the aliens; three of them, former spies, had girlfriends. But he should have known there would be Humans who wouldn't see things that way.

One of the men launched a kick Karita was too dazed to avoid. It was not so much a sharp pain he felt as a tremendous, panic-making numbness. He wondered woozily if his ribs were broken. Not that it mattered; it didn't look as if his attackers were going to stop, short of killing him. They didn't realize that they had picked one of the most unmilitary of Zentraedi; given a different one, they would have had more of a fight on their hands.

One of them drew back his heavy work boot to kick Karita again; Karita closed his eyes, waiting for the blow. But the sudden sound of shoe leather sliding on pavement and the thud of a falling body made him re-open them.

He looked up to see one of the assailants down and the other two turning to face an interloper.

Max Sterling didn't look like the conventional image of a Veritech ace. The brilliant Robotech Defense Force flier was slender, wore blue-tinted aviator glasses—with *corrective* lenses—and dyed his hair blue in keeping with the current fad for wild colors.

This young RDF legend looked mild, even vulnerable. In a time of crisis Max had risen from obscurity to dazzle humanity *and* the Zentraedi with his matchless combat flying. But that hadn't changed his basic humility and self-effacing good-naturedness.

"No more," Max told the assailants quietly. The bully on the ground shook his head angrily. Max stepped between the other two, went to Karita's side and knelt, offering his hand.

Minmei's Aunt Lena had watched the ominous trio follow Karita when he left the White Dragon; it had taken her a few minutes to find Sterling, so Max said, "Sorry I'm a little late."

This bookish-looking young man who held the highest kill score of any combat pilot in the ship offered the Zentraedi his hand. "D' you think you can stand?"

The attacker Max had floored was back on his feet, eyeing Max's RDF uniform. "You have two seconds to butt out of this, kid."

Max rose and turned, leaving Karita sitting against the wall. He took off his glasses and dropped them into Karita's limp hand.

"I guess there's gonna be a fight here, so let's get one thing straight: In case you missed the news, this man isn't our enemy. Now, are you going to let us by or what?"

Of course not. They had looked at Karita and automatically thought, *We can take him!* And that had decided the matter. Now here was the pale, unimposing Max, and their assessment was the same: *We can take him, too. No sweat.*

So the one Max had knocked down came at him first, while the others fanned out on either side.

Max didn't wait. He ducked under a powerful, slow haymaker and struck with the heel of his hand, breaking the first one's nose. A second attacker, a thick-bodied man in coveralls, hooked his fist around with all his might, but Max simply wasn't there. Dodging like a ghost, he landed a solid jab to the man's nose, bloodying it, and stepped out of the way as he staggered.

There wasn't much fighting room, and Max's usual style involved plenty of movement. But it didn't matter very much this time; he didn't want to leave Karita unprotected.

The third vigilante, younger, leaner, and faster than the other two, swung doubled fists at him from behind. Max avoided the blow, adding momentum with a quick, hard tug so that the man went toppling to his knees. Then Max spun precisely so that he had his back nearly up against the first attacker and rammed his elbow back.

The man's breath rushed out of him as he clutched his midsection. Max snapped a fist back into his face, then turned to plant a sidelong kick to the gut of the one in the coveralls. The incredible reflexes and speed that served him so well in dogfights were plain: He was difficult to see, much less hit or avoid. Karita had struggled to his feet. "Stop!"

The three attackers were battered up a bit, but the

fight had barely started. Max wasn't even breathing hard.

"No more fighting," Karita labored, clutching his side. "Hasn't there been enough?"

The first man wiped blood from a swelling lip, studying Max; indicating Karita with a toss of his head, he said, "Him and his kind killed my son. I don't care what you—"

"Look at this," Max said quietly. He displayed the RDF patch on his uniform, a diamond with curved sides like a fighting kite. "You think *I* don't understand? But listen: *He's* out of the war. Just like *I* want to be and *you* want to be.

"But we're never going to have peace unless we put the damn war behind us! So drop it, all right? Or else, c'mon: Let's finish this thing."

The first man was going to come at him again, but the other two grabbed his shoulders from either side. The young one said, "All right—for now."

Max supported Karita with his shoulder, and the three men stepped aside to let them pass. There was a tense moment as the pilot and the injured alien walked between the attackers; one of them shifted his weight, as if reconsidering his decision.

But he thought better of it and held his place, saying, "What about you, flyboy? You're goin' out there again to fight 'em, aren't ya? To kill 'em if ya can?"

Max knew that Karita was staring at him, but he answered. "Yeah. Maybe I'll wind up killing somebody a lot like your son tonight. Or he'll wind up killing me. Who knows?"

Max put Karita into a cab and sent him to the temporary quarters where the defectors were housed. He didn't have time to go along; he was late for duty as it was.

Waiting for another cab, Max gazed around at the rebuilt city of Macross. Overhead, the Enhanced Video Emulation system had created the illusion of a Terran night sky, blocking out the view of a distant alloy ceiling.

It had been a long time since Max or any of the SDF-1's other inhabitants had seen the real thing. He was already defying the odds, having survived so many combats. The EVE illusion was nice, but he hoped he'd get to see the true sky and hills and oceans of Earth again before his number came up.

Elsewhere on the SDF-1, two women rode in an uncomfortable silence on an elevator descending to a hangar deck, watching the level indicators flash.

Commander Lisa Hayes, the ship's First Officer, wasn't at ease with many people. But Lieutenant Claudia Grant, standing now with arms folded and avoiding Lisa's gaze as Lisa avoided hers, had been a close friend —perhaps Lisa's only true friend—for years.

Lisa tried to lighten the gloom. "Well, here I go again. Off for another skirmish with the brass."

That was certainly putting the best face on it. No previous effort had convinced the United Earth Defense Council to either begin peace negotiations with the Zentraedi invaders or allow the SDF-1 and its civilian refugees to return home. Lisa had volunteered to try again, to present shocking new evidence that had just emerged and exert all the pressure she could on her father, Admiral Hayes, to get him to see reason and then persuade the rest of the UEDC.

Claudia looked up. They were an odd pair: Claudia, tall and exotic-looking, several years older than Lisa, with skin the color of dark honey; and Lisa, pallid and slender, rather plain-looking until one looked a little closer.

Claudia tried to smile, running a hand through her tight brown curls. "I don't know whether it'll help or not to say this, but stop looking so grim. Girl, you remind me of the captain of a sinking ship when he finds out they forgot to bring along lifeboats. It's gonna be hard to change people's minds like that. Besides, all they can do is say 'no' again."

There was a lot more to it than that, of course. Admiral Hayes was not likely to let his only child leave Earth —to return to the SDF-1 and the endless Zentraedi attacks—once she was in the vast UEDC headquarters. Neither Claudia nor Lisa had mentioned that they would probably never see each other again.

"Yeah, I guess," Lisa said, as the doors opened and the noise and heat of the hangar deck flooded in.

The two women stepped out into a world of harsh work lights. Combat and other craft were parked everywhere, crammed in tightly with wings and ailerons folded for more efficient storage.

Maintenance crews were swarming over Veritechs damaged in the most recent fighting, while ordnance people readied ships slated for the next round of patrols and surveillance flights. The SDF-1's survival depended in large part on the Veritechs; but they would have been useless if not for the unflagging, often round-the-clock work of the men and women who repaired and serviced and rearmed them and others who risked their lives on the flight deck catapult crews.

Welding sparks flew; ordnance loader servos whined, lifting missiles and ammunition into place. Claudia had to raise her voice to be heard. "Have you told Rick about the trip or have you been too busy to see him?"

Busy had nothing to do with it, and they both knew it. Lisa had concluded that her love for Rick Hunter, leader of the Veritech Skull Team, was one-sided. By leaving the SDF-1 on a vital mission, she was also almost certainly giving up any chance of ever changing that.

"I thought I'd call him from the shuttle," she said.

Claudia exercised tremendous restraint and did not blurt out, "Lisa, stop being such a coward!" Because Lisa wasn't—she had the decorations to prove it. But where emotions were concerned, the SDF-1's competent and capable First Officer always seemed to prefer hiding under a rock someplace.

The shuttle was near the aircraft elevator–air lock that would lift it to the flight deck. Lisa's gear and the evidence she hoped would sway Admiral Hayes and the others at the UEDC were already aboard. The crew chief was running a final prelaunch check.

"The shuttle is nearly ready for launch, Captain," a female enlisted-rating tech reported. "Takeoff in ten minutes."

Captain Henry Gloval crossed the bridge to glance at several other displays, stroking his thick mustache. "Any signs of Zentraedi activity in our area?"

Vanessa answered crisply, "There's been absolutely no contact, no activity at all."

The stupendous Zentraedi armada still shadowed and prowled around the wandering battle fortress. Time and again the aliens had attacked, but in comparatively insignificant numbers. The defectors' information was only now beginning to shed light on the reasons behind that.

"There's been nothing at all?" Gloval asked again, eyes flicking across the readouts and displays. "Mm. I hope this doesn't mean they're planning an attack." He turned and paced back toward the command chair, a tall, erect figure in the high-rolled collar of his uniform jacket, hat pulled low over his eyes. He clenched his cold, empty briar in his teeth. "I don't like it, not a bit."

Lisa was his highly valued First Officer, but she was also much like a daughter to him. It had taken every bit of his reason and sense of duty to convince himself she was the logical one for this mission.

The first enlisted tech turned to Kim Young, who was manning a position nearby. She knew that Kim and the two other enlisted regulars on the bridge watch, Sammie and Vanessa, were known as the Terrible Trio, part of what amounted to a family with Gloval, Lisa Hayes, and Claudia Grant.

"Kim, does the skipper always get this...concerned?"

Kim, an elfin-faced woman wearing her dark hair in a pixie cut, showed a secret grin. She whispered, "Most of the time he's a rock. But he's worried about Lisa, and, well, there's Sammie."

Sammie Porter, youngest of the Terrible Trio, was a high-energy twenty-year-old with a thick mane of blond hair. She usually didn't know the meaning of fear...but she usually didn't know the meaning of tact, either. She was conscientious and bright but sometimes excitable.

Lisa's departure had meant a reshuffling of jobs on her watch, and Sammie had ended up with a lot of the coordinating duties Claudia and Lisa would have ordinarily handled.

"Yellow Squad, please go to preassigned coordinates before requesting computer readout," she ordered a unit of attack mecha over the comcircuit. The mammoth Robotech war machines were part of the ship's defensive force. Excaliburs and Spartans and Raidar Xs, they were like some hybrid of armored knight and walking battleship. They were among the units that guarded the ship itself, while the Veritechs sortied out into space.

Gloval bent close to check on what she was doing. "Everything all right? No trouble, I hope."

Sammie whirled and snapped, "Captain, please! I have to concentrate on these transmissions before they pile up!" Then she went back to ordering the lumbering mecha around, making sure the gun turrets and missile batteries were alert and that all intel data and situation reports were up to date.

Gloval straightened, clamping his pipe in his teeth again. "Sorry. I didn't mean to interrupt." Kim and Vanessa gave him subtle looks, barely perceptible nods to let him know that Sammie was on top of things.

Gloval had come to accept Sammie's occasional lack of diplomacy as a component of her fierce dedication to duty. Sometimes she reminded him of a small, not-to-be-trifled-with sheepdog.

Gloval considered the Terrible Trio for a moment. Through some joke of the gods, it had been *these* three whom the original Zentraedi spies—Bron, Konda, and Rico—had met and, not to put too fine a point on it, begun dating and formed attachments with.

The normally clear lines between personal life and matters of concern to the service were becoming quite muddied. The Zentraedi seemed decent enough, but there were already reports of ugly incidents between the defectors and some of the SDF-1's inhabitants. Gloval worried about the Terrible Trio, worried about the Zentraedi—was apprehensive that, after all, the two races could never coexist.

On top of that, he couldn't shake the feeling that he ought to be setting curfews, or providing chaperones, or doing *something* paternal. These things troubled him in the brief moments when he wasn't doing his best to see that his entire command wasn't obliterated.

"Shuttle escort flight, prepare for launch, five minutes," Sammie said, bent over her console. She turned to Gloval.

"Shuttle's ready, sir. Lisa will be leaving in four minutes, fifty seconds."

ABOUT THE AUTHOR

Jack McKinney has been a psychiatric aide, fusion-rock guitarist and session man, worldwide wilderness guide, and "consultant" to the U.S. Military in Southeast Asia (although they had to draft him for that).

His numerous other works of mainstream and science fiction—novels, radio and television scripts—have been written under various pseudonyms.

He resides in Ubud, on the Indonesian island of Bali.